She'd gone to bed with Marcus!

But that was too prosaic a way to describe what had happened between them. To Ann, it had been a revelation. Like seeing color television for the first time, or discovering the secret of creation. The problem was, she had no idea what to say to him now.

Hello, lover? She didn't have the nerve.

And then a gentle finger was pulling up her eyelid. Marcus peered in and asked, "Are you in there?"

His ridiculous query effectively shattered the panic that held Ann captive. Their having made love hadn't changed Marcus. He was behaving normally. At least, normally for him.

Smiling slowly, Ann opened her eyes and gave him what she hoped was a seductive look. "Of course I'm in here," she whispered. "Do you think I'd leave just when things were getting good?"

Judith McWilliams has been a published author since 1983, when she wrote her first romance. Many books later, she's still coming up with stories as fresh and funny as *Serendipity*. Our hero, incidentally, appears by popular demand—he was the ex-husband of another McWilliams heroine.

A long-time resident of beautiful New York State, Judith has recently moved into a new home with her husband and four children.

Books by Judith McWilliams

HARLEQUIN TEMPTATION
 78–POLISHED WITH LOVE
103–IN GOOD FAITH

Serendipity

JUDITH McWILLIAMS

Harlequin Books

TORONTO • NEW YORK • LONDON
AMSTERDAM • PARIS • SYDNEY • HAMBURG
STOCKHOLM • ATHENS • TOKYO • MILAN

Published August 1986

ISBN 0-373-25219-6

Printed in Canada

1

"IT'S A GOOD THING one of us likes peanut butter, Serendipity." Ann Somerton pushed a crumb of her leftover sandwich between the bars of the mouse's cage, smiling as he grabbed it.

"I don't know how you can bear to touch that thing!" Gladys Farber shuddered, her double chin shaking in revulsion. "It's disgusting. They're all disgusting." She waved her pudgy hand around the large lab with its rows and rows of caged white mice.

"No, he's not," Ann replied calmly. "I think he's kind of cute. And smart, too. I noticed it the first time I ever saw him. Remember?"

"Remember! I'm not likely to forget your opening your lunch bag and finding that . . . that thing wallowing in your cottage cheese."

"It was a mess, wasn't it?" Ann chuckled at the memory. "He had curds stuck everywhere. Didn't you, handsome?" She gently rubbed his back.

"That was no reason for you to spend your dinner hour giving him a bath, and as for using my hair dryer to dry him—" Gladys broke off in indignation.

"But I couldn't leave the poor little thing wet. He'd have caught his death of cold in all this air-conditioning."

"You should have turned him in to the head of the lab. It wasn't your fault that some technician left his cage open and he got loose."

"I couldn't do that." Ann's hand hovered protectively over his tiny head. "This isn't just any mouse, I'll have you know. Serendipity is the Tom Selleck of mousedom."

"Tom Selleck!"

"Uh-huh." Ann's dark brown eyes gleamed with laughter. "It's his expression. I suspect that underneath his white fur beats the heart of a macho mouse."

"He's a runt," Gladys stated flatly, "and once they start using him in one of their experiments, he's not gonna last long."

"Probably not." A brief flash of sadness touched Ann at the thought of Serendipity's inevitable end. In the three short weeks since she'd rescued him from his encounter with her cottage cheese, she'd become inordinately fond of him. For such a miniscule creature, he seemed to have a very distinct personality.

"There." Gladys gave the brown linoleum a final swipe with her mop, then squinted myopically at the clock on the opposite wall.

"Ten-forty," Ann told her.

"I can see that," Gladys lied. "Only twenty minutes left till quitting time."

"Thank God it's Friday." Ann wearily pushed a strand of light brown hair behind her ear, yawned and then stretched her slender frame to its full five foot, five inches. "I'm going to sleep till noon tomorrow." A smile of pleasure at the thought curved her soft pink lips.

"Sleep!" Gladys snorted. "It's not natural. A pretty young thing your age looking forward to the weekend so you can sleep."

"I'm twenty-seven," Ann said mildly.

"Bah, that's no age at all. Not when you get to be sixty-one like me."

"Go on," Ann teased. "You can't be sixty-one! A pretty young thing like you?"

"Quit trying to change the subject, Ann Somerton. I still say it isn't right. You ought to be looking forward to a couple of dates this weekend."

"No time." Nor any inclination, she thought ruefully. Her life was hectic enough at present without the added distraction of a man. She pushed another scrap of bread into Serendipity's cage.

"You'd have plenty of time to date if you weren't always studying," Gladys insisted. "Oh, I know you're dead set on learning to be a computer programmer. Not that I blame you. Cleaning labs is all right when you're my age and never finished the eighth grade, but it's no job for a pretty girl like you. But you don't need to wear yourself out studying to escape. All you got to do is find yourself a man to marry and let him take you away from all this."

"Haven't you heard that the modern woman doesn't sit around waiting for Prince Charming to rescue her anymore?" Ann replied with a determined lightness. "We solve our own problems."

"I still think the old ways are best," Gladys said emphatically. "Now then," she said, reverting to the work at hand, "you finish wiping down the counters in here while I run a quick sweeper over the offices at the end of the hall. Okay?"

"Sure," Ann agreed, and Gladys bustled through the door.

Ann gave Serendipity a final pat, then picked up a damp cloth and began to work her way around the room. She was almost done when the mouse's determined chatter told her that he'd finished his bread and wanted more.

"Just a minute, Serendipity." Ann dropped her rag on the cleaning cart and rinsed the strong smell of disinfectant from the roughened skin of her slim fingers.

"For the life of me, handsome, I can't see what your fascination with peanut butter is." She pushed the last bread crumb through the bars. "To tell you the truth, if it weren't so cheap and nutritious and if payday weren't five days away, I wouldn't touch the stuff with a ten-foot pole."

Serendipity ignored her as he stashed her offering in the bottom of his cage for later.

"No discrimination, that's your trouble." She gently rubbed the soft fur on his little head with her finger. "Now what would really be nice would be a thick, juicy steak with a steaming baked potato swimming in butter and sour cream." She sighed longingly at the thought.

"It won't be long now, Serendipity. Just a little over two months left of the summer session. Then the fall term and next January I'll be a full-fledged graduate of the Morrison Business School with hundreds of employers clamoring to secure my skills on the computer."

"Cherrup." Serendipity twitched his long white whiskers, and Ann giggled at his accusing look.

"Well, maybe not hundreds. But, hopefully, at least one. I'll have you know that the graduates of the Morrison Business School are in great demand. It says so right on their brochure. We—" She broke off, expecting to see Gladys as the door opened. But it wasn't her comfortable co-worker, it was a man. One she'd never seen before.

A pale yellow knit shirt was stretched across the intimidating breadth of his shoulders. Its short sleeves emphasized his well-developed biceps and strong forearms, which were liberally covered with dark hair. Worn denims hugged his narrow hips and the length of his long legs. A tattered pair of Adidas shod feet that seemed too large for his height, which Ann guessed to be about five-foot-eleven.

Imperceptibly, she edged closer to Serendipity's cage, irrationally wishing that he really were Tom Selleck. She could have used his comforting presence beside her as she faced this stranger.

Nervously, she chewed on her lower lip. It was possible he had broken into the building. She'd heard lurid tales from Gladys about junkies who'd made their way into the institute, thinking that simply because the center performed cancer research, there must be drugs lying around.

She tried to measure the distance between him and the open doorway, only to find her gaze effortlessly caught and held by his bright blue eyes.

Not a junkie. Ann's tense muscles relaxed slightly. His clear, direct stare told her that.

"Don't make a pet out of the specimen." The man's deep velvety voice matched the implied strength of his muscular body. "I'm using that row of mice in an experiment that starts tomorrow."

"Who are you?" she blurted out.

"Marcus Blackmore. I'm—" He broke off as the pager he was wearing clipped to his belt emitted a sharp beep. "Good, my phone call." He turned the sound off and left without so much as a nod to her.

Ann frowned, trying to remember exactly who Marcus Blackmore was. She'd never paid much attention to gossip about the center's staff. To her this job was strictly a means to keep from starving until her computer training was completed. But still Marcus Blackmore's name was vaguely familiar, even if his face wasn't.

There was an office door down the hall that said M. Blackmore Ph.D. M.D., she suddenly remembered. *M* for Marcus? It seemed likely that the office belonged to the man she had just met.

Ann glanced down into Serendipity's shining eyes, which were frankly pleading for more food. The poor little thing. "He won't have you," she declared with an impulsiveness totally foreign to her normally well-ordered life. "I don't care how necessary his research is or how many lives he might save someday. All I care about is your life and right now!"

Hastily, she unlatched the cage and grabbed the surprised mouse. She pushed the wire door closed and glanced around the room. She couldn't hide him in here. He'd simply wind up in another experiment. She'd have to take him home with her.

She hurried over to the cleaning cart and grabbed her straw purse, trying to work the stiff catch with one hand. It refused to yield to her frantic efforts, and she froze when she heard the sound of footsteps echoing in the hall. She shot a despairing glance at the open doorway and, abandoning her attempts to open her purse, stuffed the vociferously protesting Serendipity into the pile of clean rags on the bottom of the cart.

"No, stay there." She pushed his inquisitive nose back under a rag and dropped a few more on his head, hoping to muffle the sounds of his indignant chatter.

"Miss?"

Nervously, Ann turned to face Marcus, being careful to position her body between him and the cart.

He walked toward her with an indolent grace that bespoke a superbly conditioned body, but she was too nervous to appreciate his physique. It was imperative that she shield Serendipity from his sharp blue eyes. He paused a few feet from her and she cast a furtive glance at the bottom of the cart, her heart sinking at the sight of the rags quivering under the force of Serendipity's anger.

Surreptitiously she edged closer to the cart as she franticly tried to figure out how to get rid of him before he caught sight of the mouse.

"Gladys Moyers is in charge of the cleaning crew," Ann threw out, trying to divert him. "If you're looking for her, she's doing the offices at the end of the hall."

"I'm not," he replied calmly, setting his clipboard on the long counter to his left.

Ann took advantage of his movement to quickly check the bottom of the cleaning cart. It was not a reassuring sight. Serendipity's small head was now entirely free and, if the gleam in his outraged eyes was any indication, very shortly the rest of him would be, too. She had to do something, but what? Mesmerized, she watched in horror as Marcus turned back to her.

She took a deep breath and tried the only diversionary tactic she could think of on such short notice. Pretending to trip over her own feet, she fell toward him in the hope that he'd be so busy catching her that he wouldn't notice that the cleaning rags seemed to have a life of their own.

"Allow me." His strong hands encircled her slight waist.

Ann's breath caught in her lungs at the feel of his fingers burning through the thin cotton of her well-worn shirt. Powerful fingers. She recognized the latent strength in them as they hauled her upright, even as her mind sought to deny the trembling awareness his touch activated deep within her.

"Thanks," she muttered, disconcerted by her body's unbidden and unwanted reaction to him.

"It's quite all right." His deep voice was threaded with an amusement that set her teeth on edge. "It's the least I could do for someone who threw themself at my feet."

"I did not!" she snapped. Between nervousness at having stolen a mouse and embarrassment at the necessity of having to make a fool of herself, she was becoming rattled. Stepping back when he released her, Ann shot another glance behind her at the cart and almost groaned. Serendipity was now completely out of the rags and glaring angrily at her. Further action was definitely called for. Taking a deep breath, she again flung herself into Marcus's waiting arms, trying to make it seem as though she hadn't fully recovered her balance after the first incident.

"I must say," he commented with a chuckle, "you're either hopelessly maladroit or you've chosen a very novel method of introducing yourself, Ann Somerton." He read her name off the plastic identification card she wore clipped to her shirt.

His teasing words floated over her head, unheard. Ann was too busy trying to process the physical sensations flooding her to concentrate on what he was saying. Her face was buried in the open neck of his shirt and the crisp black hairs on his chest tickled her nose. The faint smell of soap, overlaid by the much more basic smell of the man himself, filled her nostrils. Without thinking, she breathed deeply, reveling in the heady fragrance. Her deep breath lifted her breasts into the rock-hard wall of his chest, and she could feel them swelling in pleasure at the contact.

"Ann?" His worried query effectively shattered her unexpected sexual euphoria, jerking her back to reality. She froze, not wanting to back up and see his amused face and equally not wanting to stay in his arms.

Marcus made the decision for her. His hands gripped her shoulders, and he set her back from the warm length of his body.

"I'm sorry. I was just . . . It's late." She inadvertently completed the image of scatterbrained female she'd been trying to foster. "I'm tired and hungry."

"So am I." He gave her a lopsided grin, displaying slightly crooked white teeth. "I know a diner near here. I'll buy you a snack."

"A snack!" Her mouth dropped open, and she gaped at him. She wasn't sure what kind of response she'd been expecting, but an invitation to eat definitely wasn't it.

"As in food," he said, his eyes twinkling. "Even someone as skinny as you must eat occasionally."

"I am not skinny!" she denied. "I'm fashionably slender."

"Skinny," he repeated firmly. "You need fattening up, and I know just the place to do it. Wally's Diner over on Delancey serves the best barbecued ribs you've ever tasted."

"Ribs?" Ann swallowed, the very thought of eating something besides a peanut butter sandwich filling her with longing.

"Uh-huh. And fettuccine made to order with real cream and freshly ground Parmesan cheese."

She agonized. She shouldn't go. She knew it. For one thing, she still had the problem of what to do with Serendipity and for another . . . She peered speculatively at Marcus. There was something about Marcus Blackmore, something that seemed to short-circuit the rational being she knew herself to be. Instinctively she recognized him as a danger to her hard-won peace of mind.

Don't be an idiot. She pulled her imagination up short. Her reaction to him was undoubtedly caused by a combination of embarrassment over having to pretend to be a klutz and nervousness that he might find out that she had liberated Serendipity. Marcus Blackmore was no different from any other man, and she was no different than she was twenty minutes ago.

"And fresh strawberry pie smothered in mounds of real whipped cream," continued his persuasive voice, promising untold gastronomic delights.

"I'd love to," she heard herself say.

"Good. You go put that—" he gestured toward the cleaning cart behind her and she edged closer to it "—wherever it goes while I lock up my office. I'll meet you at the front entrance in ten minutes."

"All right." Ann frowned, a feeling of déjà vu washing over her. Her ex-husband Steve used to issue orders in exactly that manner, except he had usually tacked on an irritating 'got that?'

She told herself to stop being so hypersensitive, deciding that was very good advice. There was no reason why he shouldn't tell her where to meet him. He was the one who issued the invitation, after all. She waited until Marcus had left the room, then hurriedly grabbed Serendipity and unceremoniously stuffed him into her purse, ignoring his angry chattering. If she could pretend to have two left feet, then he could put up with a ride in her purse.

"WHAT'S YOUR HURRY?" Gladys frowned over her coffee cup as Ann rushed into the employees' lounge.

"Dinner." Ann gently placed her purse on the bench in front of her locker so as not to frighten Serendipity.

"You want to be careful." Gladys frowned worriedly. "New York City's East Side is dangerous enough in the daytime for a woman on her own, but in the middle of the night . . ."

"Haven't you heard?" Ann grinned at her. "The city never sleeps."

"At least the crooks don't," Gladys replied gloomily.

"Set your mind to rest, Gladys. I won't be alone. Dr. Blackmore invited me out for a snack."

"Marcus Blackmore!" Gladys's eyes bulged. "Marvelous Marcus?"

"Marvelous Marcus?" She compared Gladys's description to the image that readily formed in her mind. A broad forehead, a sharply chiseled, faintly crooked nose, lean cheeks, an uncompromisingly square chin with a deep cleft in the middle and a wide sensuous mouth with laugh lines radiating from the corners. Yes, "marvelous" did fit him.

"Marvelous Marcus is what the cleaning staff calls him." Gladys sighed. "Oh that gorgeous black curly hair, and he's got the most soulful eyes."

"You make him sound like a cocker spaniel," Ann said, smiling, rummaging around in the top of her locker for a spare lipstick. She didn't want to use the one in her purse and risk Serendipity escaping. Gladys would never approve of mouse-napping.

"No, not a cocker spaniel." Gladys seemed to give serious consideration to Ann's words. "More like a bulldog. They say once he gets his teeth into something, he never lets go."

"I'll remember not to let him bite me. Ah, there it is." She extracted a tube of bright red lipstick.

"I'm serious," Gladys insisted, watching Ann deftly apply the glowing color to her soft lips. "What's the matter?" she demanded as Ann frowned at her image in the tiny mirror on the inside of her locker door.

"It's too bright."

"No, it isn't," Gladys disagreed. "It's cheerful and your skin looks like white satin. But that makes it even worse."

"Makes what worse?" Ann tugged the comb through her straight shoulder-length hair.

"Your dating Marvelous Marcus."

"One midnight snack does not constitute dating," Ann pointed out, laughing. "And besides, he can't be a full-fledged lecher or I'd have heard rumors about him by now."

"It's not that. It's just that he has a nasty habit of taking a woman out a few times and then forgetting all about her. He was dating a pretty blond lab technician from up on the sixth floor last year, and then he got busy with some experiment or other and never called her again. She was so upset she found herself another job. Anyway, you haven't heard of him because he's been in California for the past year. He got some highfalutin appointment to mess around in some lab or another out on the West Coast doing whatever it is he does. He must've just got back because this is the first I've heard of it. I think he only went because he was breaking his heart over his wife." Gladys pursed her lips sagely.

"He's married?" Ann tried to ask casually, ignoring the strange sinking feeling that seized her stomach.

"He was. Years ago when I first came to work here, but they got a divorce."

"Oh." Ann released her breath on a long sigh. "Well, I can't vouch for Marcus, but you don't have to worry about me. It's a long way from a snack to a broken heart. Have a nice weekend, Gladys, and I'll see you on Monday." She carefully picked up her purse.

"Just make sure that you don't bite off more than you can chew!" Gladys always got in the last word.

Marcus Blackmore was certainly mouthwatering, Ann mused. Pausing near the staff door, she cautiously eyed Marcus who was standing in the brilliantly lit outer lobby of the institute. All her uncertainties about the wisdom of accepting his invitation came rushing back. Beside the fact that his presence seemed to immerse her in a time warp, propelling her backward to the emotional uncertainty of early adolescence, he was quite simply outside her very limited experience with men.

What did you talk about with a man as well educated as Marcus Blackmore? For a second, alarm paralyzed her mind, but she firmly squelched the panic. She wasn't dumb. She had a college degree, even if it was in classic languages, she reminded herself. That should allow her to hold her own with anyone. Well, almost anyone. Her eyes came back to rest on Marcus, and she apprehensively twisted a lock of her silky hair.

She didn't need to actually discuss anything scientific with him, she finally decided. All she had to do was to ask him a few leading questions. Men were supposed to be eager to deliver long monologues about both themselves and their work. A shiver of uncertainty skipped across her mind. Somehow she doubted that Marcus was ever going to fit into some neat, little preconceived niche. But it didn't matter, she assured herself. What mattered was that she was starving, and he was willing to buy her a meal.

"Come on, Serendipity." Ann gently patted the side of her purse. Taking a deep breath, she crossed the lobby toward the waiting Marcus. No matter how awkward talking to him proved to be, it would be worth it to get a taste of something besides peanut butter.

"KEEP THE CHANGE." Marcus handed a bill across the back seat to the cabbie as the taxi stopped in front of a brightly lit diner.

"Thanks, mister. You have yourself a good night." He gave a lascivious wink that made Ann long to hit him over the head with her purse until she remembered Serendipity. What was it about men that made them see every woman under ninety as a challenge to their libido! But if Marcus caught the cabbie's innuendo, he ignored it. Opening the door, he stepped out.

Ann scooted across the seat to follow him, freezing when the faint echo of a disgruntled "cherrup" reached her ears. Hurriedly, she shifted her purse to her other side, interposing her body between Marcus and the telltale noise. It didn't help. With a silent apology to the liberated woman she knew herself to be, she pretended to teeter, using her movement as an excuse to give her purse an admonitory shake, hoping to silence Serendipity.

Marcus encircled her waist with a muscular arm and pulled her into his side, steadying her slight frame against him.

"I..." She automatically began to move away, but his arm tightened, melding her slight curves into the solid planes of his body.

"Woman, I can't decide if you're tired, or hungry, or just plain clumsy. But I do know I'll feel a lot better once I get you inside and safely sitting down."

"I am not clumsy," she said in perfect truth, vainly trying to shut her mind to the persuasive feel of his solid frame. It was an exercise in futility. The pressure of his hard thigh pushing against her much softer one and the secure warmth of his encircling arm melted her resolve not to respond. She took a deep breath and tried to regain control of herself, not even noticing when the cabbie, with another wink and a thumbs-up gesture to Marcus, pulled away. She sighed, wishing that she'd been quick-witted enough to have figured out more dignified a way of rescuing Serendipity.

"I promise not to fall all over you again," she said carefully.

"You misunderstand me." His lips twitched with suppressed laughter as he moved back a step. "I'm not objecting to your throwing yourself at me. It's where you pick to do it that's the problem. Now, if you'd like to get a take-out order of ribs and eat them at my place, I promise not to make a single complaint."

"If we went to your place, I have the feeling that I'd be the one with the cause for complaint," she said tartly.

"I don't think so." He seemed to give her words serious consideration. "At least, I've never had any complaints before. But if you did have one, I'd certainly be willing to keep working on it until I got it right."

"I'll save you the trouble. We'll eat here," Ann replied, uncertain of his mood. Although his words had been uttered in a solemn tone, there had been a fugitive twinkle deep in his azure eyes.

"Don't be too considerate." Marcus opened the door to the diner and, with an unaffected courtly gesture, motioned her inside. Ann felt a warm surge of happiness course through her body. She suddenly felt alive and desirable and very conscious of her feminity. A feminity that for the past nine months seemed to have been buried under the demands of her hectic schedule.

The bored-looking waitress behind the cash register shifted a wad of gum from one side of her mouth to the other and asked, "Two?"

"Yes," Marcus confirmed.

"Counter okay?" The woman gestured toward the right side of the diner, which was taken up by a long counter and a row of red vinyl-covered chrome stools.

Ann noted the distance between the stools. Her purse would be right under Marcus's nose and, more importantly, his ears. Remembering Serendipity's chatter she decided, no, definitely not the counter.

"I'd prefer a table." She smiled at the woman.

"Sure, lady." A careless hand waved toward the row of tables, which were almost empty. "As you can see, we haven't exactly got a run on 'em."

"Thanks." Ann shot a furtive glance at Marcus as they made their way toward the back, wondering if he minded her speaking up. His impassive face gave her no clue. She slid into a patched red vinyl booth and gently deposited her purse on the floor at her feet, hoping that all the unaccustomed movement hadn't made Serendipity sick.

"What would you like?" Marcus asked. "Ribs, spoon bread, fettuccine, strawberry pie?"

"Yes," she sighed happily.

"Yes, what?"

"Yes everything. Unless . . ." Her voice trailed away as a horrible thought suddenly struck her, and she frowned uncertainly at Marcus. Perhaps he was short of cash. How did one go about asking a man if he could afford what you wanted to order? She'd never come up against this problem before. When she and her ex-husband had dined out, he would simply tell her how much money they had and she'd tailor her wants accordingly. But she could hardly ask a virtual stranger how much he had to spend. Nor, considering the fragile state of her finances until payday, could she offer to pay herself.

"Unless what?" he asked, watching the emotions flit across her face.

"It is kind of late to eat very much," she floundered. "And I'm not sure . . . I mean . . ." Nervously she moistened her lower lip, wishing she had the experience necessary to handle a situation like this. "Why don't you order for me?" she finally said, deciding that he'd hardly be likely to order something he couldn't pay for.

"Why would you . . ." He stared thoughtfully at her, and then an incredulous expression lit his eyes. "Ann Somerton, are you actually worried about my being hauled in for defrauding an innkeeper!"

"No!" she snapped, embarrassed at having her motivation exposed. "I'm worried about my winding up washing dishes."

"Well, let's set your mind at ease." He calmly reached into his hip pocket, extracted a worn leather wallet and pulled out a wad of bills.

"Dr. Blackmore!" she admonished casting a swift glance around the diner. The waitress was eyeing her with envious approval. "Stop that!"

"Marcus," he told her. "Call me Marcus."

She took immediate exception to his pronouncement. "Lo, I have spoken!"

"You don't like Marcus?" he queried. "That certainly isn't an insurmountable problem." He stopped counting the bills and cocked his head to one side as if considering a solution. "I'm afraid my middle name is out. I couldn't take being called Mortimer over any period of time."

"Yes, I can understand that." Ann nodded, wondering if his comment meant that he planned to ask her out again. She ignored the sharp stab of pleasure the thought brought. "I wasn't objecting to your name. I was objecting to the overbearing way you calmly ordered me to call you Marcus."

"Oh?" He blinked at her charge, obviously taken aback. "But how should I have indicated that I wanted you to call me Marcus?"

Ann looked into his puzzled blue eyes, wondering if he was mocking her. He didn't seem to be. Deciding to accept his question at face value, she said, "Well, you could have politely requested that I call you by your first name."

"Politely?" He frowned.

"You know, words like please and thank you? That kind of politely."

"If that's what you want," he said with the air of an adult humoring a fractious child. "I would greatly appreciate it if you could bring yourself to call me by my given name. If you please," he added as an afterthought.

"You're right," she conceded. "'Call me Marcus' sounds much better."

"I usually am." He smiled smugly and went back to counting his bills, leaving Ann simmering with frustration. She wasn't even sure who had won that exchange.

"Marcus . . ." she began.

"Just a second. I'm checking to see whether or not I can afford you."

She opened her mouth to retort and then noticed the silently waiting waitress. If the conspiratorial wink she gave Ann was any indication, she had heard Marcus's last comment.

Ann briefly closed her eyes and resisted an impulse to crawl under the table. How on earth had she come to be sitting in a run-down diner in the middle of the night with a world-renowned biochemist who was fast shattering all her preconceived ideas about stuffy, staid scientists? Her normally well-organized, nothing-left-to-chance life-style had definitely been thrown for a loop.

"Four hundred seventeen dollars and thirty-two cents," he announced. "Is that enough?"

"Yes." Recklessly Ann grinned at him, oblivious to what the waitress thought. As long as she was here, she intended to enjoy herself. Tomorrow she'd slip back onto the safe predictable path she'd chosen for herself.

2

ANN SIGHED, UTTERLY REPLETE, and then considered the huge piece of strawberry pie in front of her. It looked luscious with its glazed red berries peeking up through clouds of whipped cream. Regretfully she laid her napkin down beside her plate of bare rib bones. Much as she wanted to, there was no way she could possibly eat dessert.

"Done?" Marcus asked in amusement. "Surely you aren't going to allow the pie to escape!"

"I was hungry," she excused herself.

"From the looks of things, you were bordering on starvation," he said wryly. "I haven't seen food disappear that fast since my sixteen-year-old cousin spent the weekend with me last year."

"It's healthy to have a good appetite."

"It certainly bodes well for your enjoyment of other pleasures of the flesh."

His slow smile reached out to engulf her, and she felt her heart lurch. She blinked to break the spell he was weaving and scrabbled for a safer line of conversation. "You've been in California, haven't you?" she asked.

"Yes," Marcus affirmed with a nod.

"I've heard the sunshine's lovely out there," she tried again.

"It's tempered with mud slides and brush fires."

"What kind of research were you doing?" Doggedly she asked another leading question.

"Cancer," he answered succinctly.

Ann closed her eyes in exasperation. "Listen, my friend, I don't think that you quite understand the dynamics of this situation."

"Of course I do. It's food." He glanced down at her empty plate with its pile of bare rib bones. "Or rather, it was."

"Of course it isn't," she muttered, vaguely embarrassed by the evidence of how much she'd eaten.

"You mean it really is sex?" His eyes narrowed with sudden interest.

"Sex?" she parroted.

"Mmm, I was reading a paper by a psychiatrist who claimed that all relationships between a man and a woman were motivated by sexual desire. That there was no such thing as an asexual working relationship between a man and a woman. Or even friendship for that matter."

"Sounds like a rather sweeping statement to me," Ann said dismissively, having no desire to discuss the subject. She was already much too aware of him as a sexual being.

Rushing into speech when he opened his mouth, she pointed out, "Anyway, I was referring to the dynamics of the conversation." She was beginning to understand what Gladys had meant, likening him to a bulldog. If she didn't want to wind up discussing sex, then she'd better divert him—fast. "And it isn't going to prosper unless you can bring yourself to answer in a little more detail than with single words."

"Maybe sex will prosper instead?" He managed to sound boyishly hopeful. A circumstance that Ann instinctively mistrusted. Marcus Blackmore wasn't boyishly anything. He was a man, a very determined man.

"Not a chance."

"Pity," he sighed. "It had a lot more scope, but if conversation is all there is, we'll have to give it another shot. Why are you cleaning out the labs?"

"Because the center pays me, of course."

"So would a lot of other employers. I would think you'd want a job with more challenge to it."

"All in good time." Ann sipped her coffee. "What you're forgetting is that you just can't walk into interesting jobs with scope. You have to have a skill, and after eight years of being a housewife, the only marketable talent I have is for cleaning things."

"No formal education?" he asked sympathetically.

"Oh, I've got a degree for all the good it does me." She shrugged. "There isn't much call in the labor market for Greek scholars. Not even with Latin thrown in."

"So why didn't you study something more practical," he asked reasonably.

"A combination of lack of foresight and self-indulgence," she admitted. "I started on my degree right after I was married, and since my husband was vehemently opposed to working wives and since I loved Greek anyway, I majored in classical languages. When I was divorced and had to earn my own living, I went back to school to learn to be a computer programmer. You don't approve?" Ann asked curiously when he frowned.

"Of your studying, yes. Of computers, most definitely not. They're anathema."

"They are not," she insisted. "They're simply machines."

"They're fiends! Last year the institute gave me a small computer to use, and I spent one whole weekend putting information into it."

"So?"

"Then, when its memory banks were full, the damn thing ate all the data! If this were a more enlightened age, computers would be burned at the stake for the devils they are."

"That's a very common attitude." She nodded sagely. "Man has been blaming machines for his own mistakes since the first cavemen's stone came off his hachet."

"I did not make a mistake!" He was outraged. "I followed the directions exactly."

"If you had followed the directions, it would have worked. Computers don't have original thoughts. They simply obey a series of set commands."

"It isn't natural," he complained. "A nice woman like you siding with those things."

"I happen to like computers. They do exactly what you tell them to. They don't change the rules on you halfway through the game."

"Somehow that comment sounds fraught with psychological meaning." Marcus eyed her thoughtfully.

"What?" she scoffed. "Simply because I like things to progress in a nice orderly sequence. It's much neater."

"But people aren't neat."

"We weren't talking about people. We were talking about computers."

"Were we?" He studied her with an intensity that set alarm bells ringing in her mind. This man was far too astute. He was trained to delve beneath the surface for the less obvious answers, and the speculative look on his face made her very uneasy. She most definitely didn't want him probing behind the serene front she presented to the world. With an inward sigh of relief, Ann saw the waitress amble over, an almost empty coffeepot held in her hand.

"Fill up?" the woman queried.

Ann looked at the thick black dregs swirling around the bottom of the pot and just managed to suppress a shudder.

Marcus glanced questioningly at Ann. When she shook her head, he declined, also.

"Would you please bring us a carryout container for the pie?" he asked.

"We don't do carryouts," the woman stated emphatically. "This isn't a hamburger joint, you know."

"Indeed, we do." He gave her a gleaming white smile. "In fact, that's the trouble. The main course was so delicious that we ate too much, and it would be criminal to waste something as delectable as your pie."

"Yah, it would, wouldn't it?" She thawed perceptibly in the face of such blatant flattery. "I guess I could give you the empty pie tin," she offered. "If you're careful, you shouldn't have any trouble."

"Thank you." He rewarded the woman with a beaming smile.

"Thank you." Ann told him once the woman had left.

"You can thank me later." His words were innocuous, but the gleam in his eyes told another story.

Ann felt a nervous leap in the region of her heart, which she tried to ignore. The problem was that it had been so long since she'd had an active social life. Almost ten years and then she'd been a shy seventeen, dating equally shy teenage boys. She had absolutely no experience in dealing with someone like Marcus Blackmore. She should have had, she thought bitterly. If she had had the sense to learn something about the world and herself before she'd entered the institution of marriage, then handling someone like Marcus would have been second nature to her by now.

"Don't look so sad." He misunderstood her bleak expression. "She's found the pie plate."

"So she has." Ann smiled, forcing down the unaccustomed feelings this man's presence engendered. She wasn't sure if it were merely the fact that this was her first date in almost a year or whether it was something about Marcus Blackmore himself that affected her so strangely. But whatever it was, it was a complication she would have preferred to avoid.

"Here you are." The waitress slid the pie onto the clean aluminum tin and set it in front of Ann.

"Thank you," Ann murmured.

"And here's the bill." The woman handed Marcus the crumpled green check and leaned a hand on the table while he reached for his wallet.

Ann blinked tiredly, stifled a yawn, then sniffed. The frigid air in the diner was beginning to make her nose drip. She unzipped her purse to get a Kleenex and then froze when a tiny pink nose with angrily twitching whiskers popped out.

Ann glanced quickly at Marcus, but he was busy paying the check. She couldn't believe she'd forgotten a basic thing like the mouse in her purse. Quickly she reached for him, but it was too late. Serendipity was tired of being imprisoned, and he'd suddenly seen his chance to do something about it. Under Ann's horrified eyes, he ran down the strap of her purse and headed across the table.

Abandoning discretion, Ann made a grab for him and missed. Serendipity swerved to avoid capture and ran across the waitress's hand.

"Rats!" The woman let out a piercing scream and began to shake her hand in violent repudiation of the feel of his tiny feet.

"Don't hurt him," Ann yelled, ignoring the incredulous look in Marcus's eyes as Serendipity skittered down the table leg.

"What the hell was that!" he demanded.

"Rats, rats!" the waitress answered him, if somewhat inaccurately. "We're inundated with rats."

"One mouse does not an inundation make," Ann observed tritely, but no one was listening to her. The waitress climbed onto a chair, still shrieking at the top of her lungs, and Marcus took off after Serendipity.

Ann looked from the screaming woman to Marcus, who was scrambling around the table legs after the mouse, and couldn't decide whether to laugh or cry. The whole scene was like something out of a Three Stooges movie. She tried to think, but the waitress's yelling was playing havoc with her sleepy mind. That and her fear of what Marcus was going to say about her theft.

"There's a gun in the cash register," the waitress yelled. "Shoot it!"

Her words broke through the inertia that seemed to hold Ann captive.

"Shoot him! Are you nuts!" Ann yelled back at the woman. "All this fuss over one little mouse."

Ann turned in time to see Marcus lunge around a stool in pursuit of the obviously confused Serendipity. She winced as Marcus misjudged the distance and hit his head on the corner of the counter with a sickening thud. She watched in horror as his eyes slid shut and he slumped sideways.

"Marcus!" She jumped out of her seat, breathing a sigh of relief when he groaned and gingerly touched his black hair.

"Dammit!" he swore, shaking his head in an attempt to clear his vision.

Serendipity, apparently feeling he'd just vanquished the foe, skated across the floor and landed in a heap on Ann's worn loafers.

"You poor little thing." Ann hurriedly picked him up before he took off again. "Did those nasty, big people frighten you?" She glanced from the waitress, who was slowly turning purple, to Marcus, who was rubbing his forehead in a dazed manner, and decided that this definitely qualified as one of those times when discretion was the better part of valor.

She shoved the chastised Serendipity back into her purse and slung it over her shoulder. The bright red of the glistening strawberry pie caught her eye and, without taking time to think, she grabbed the pie pan and hurried out, anxious to remove herself from the scene.

Marcus was all right, she placated her conscience. He was merely stunned by that crack on his head, and she most emphatically didn't want to try to explain Serendipity to him until he'd had a chance to cool down. Say in three or four months.

Ann paused in front of the restaurant, trying to figure out exactly where she was in relation to her apartment. She knew the diner was on Delancey, and since they'd only come a few blocks off Broadway she was probably on the outskirts of Little Italy. Briefly she closed her eyes and tried to picture a map. If she had the diner placed correctly, then she was a good distance south of her own efficiency on Twenty-ninth Street. Certainly too far to walk, especially at night. She glanced up the street, brightening when she saw a cruising cab. She really couldn't afford it, but right now money was the least of her worries. She needed to get out of here before Marcus demanded Serendipity back. Ann raised her arm and gestured madly, breathing a sigh of relief when the cabbie acknowledged her.

Her hand was on the door handle when she felt strong fingers close like a vise around her upper arm. Tensely she peered over her shoulder, shrinking under Marcus's furious glare.

"Oh, hi," she said brightly, and then winced at the absolute insanity of the remark. Apparently Marcus wasn't too impressed, either, for his grip tightened and he bit out, "Get into that damn cab."

"I'm getting, I'm getting," she muttered, strangely not the least bit afraid of the rather formidable anger he was displaying. Somehow she knew that he would never knowingly inflict pain on another human being. She just wished she had a little clearer reading on how he felt about verbal abuse.

Ann stumbled into the cab, plopped down on the musty-smelling seat and placed the piece of pie beside her in the hope of forcing some distance between herself and Marcus. Unfortunately, it didn't work out that way. In the dim light of the cab's interior, he didn't see the pie and landed directly on it.

Ann registered the ominous sound of crinkling tin foil with a fatalistic calm. Of course he'd landed on the pie. It had been that kind of an evening from start to finish.

"What was that I just sat on?" Marcus demanded, his voice tight.

"Nothin', buddy. I run a clean cab."

"He's talking about my strawberry pie," Ann told the cabbie.

"Strawberry pie?" The very mildness of Marcus's query made her want to open the door and run for it, but she resisted the impulse. She didn't know him well enough to predict his reaction. He might take it in his head to chase her, and undoubtedly he would catch her. She recalled the taut feel of his lithe body. Here, the cabbie's presence would act as a curb on Marcus's more aggressive instincts. At least she certainly hoped so.

"You remember," she babbled on in the face of his silence, "the one with all the whipped cream on it that I was going to have for breakfast." To her dismay, she heard a faintly accusatory note creep into her voice.

"What's with you two?" the cabbie demanded. "I haven't any time for no funny business."

"Sitting on a piece of pie is not funny! St. Luke's Place, the Village," Marcus snapped the address at the man.

"All right. I'll take you, but it's going to cost you extra for the mess," warned the cabbie.

"The mess is on me, not on this musty, mildewed heap, which is undoubtedly harboring every form of microbe known to man!" Marcus bit out.

"There's no call to get uppity with me, bud." The cabbie pulled the taxi out into the sparse traffic with a rubber-laying shriek. "It isn't my fault you sat on the lady's pie. You should learn to keep your eyes open."

Ann automatically held her breath, waiting for the inevitable explosion. To her surprise, his response was forbearing.

"You're undoubtedly right. If I'm going to survive around Calamity Jane here, I'm going to need all my senses working overtime."

The cabbie chortled. "That's women, buddy. Where would we be without the little darlins."

"Where indeed," Marcus muttered under his breath.

Ann leaned back and watched the winking lights of Broadway flash by while she tried to think. The address Marcus had given the cabbie in Greenwich Village wasn't for her apartment, so presumably it was for his. But where did that leave her? If he intended to send her home alone after he got out, she hoped he would prepay the fare. The sound of the meter ticking over made her wince. If she got stuck with the bill, she'd be lucky even to get peanut butter to eat until payday.

Maybe he intended to take her home with him and try to seduce her. For a wild moment a heady combination of excitement, fear and outrage filled her before common sense intruded. She simply wasn't the type of woman men dragged off to seduce. Not even at her best, and no one could claim she was at her best right now. Dressed in old clothes and having just spent eight hours cleaning dusty labs, she was tired and dirty. Not a combination to inspire uncontrollable lust in a man. Especially, not a man as sophisticated as Marcus. Besides, she consoled herself, Marcus wasn't in particularly good shape himself right now. She swallowed a giggle at the thought of his strawberry-stained pants.

Firmly, she focused her attention on the three-story brownstones lining the street. Some were huge, some small, but all were in excellent repair. There was none of the faint air of decay that hung over the houses in her own neighborhood; this area was solid and substantial. Rather like Marcus himself, she decided, the imaginative comparison flickered through her mind.

"Two houses up on the right." Marcus instructed.

The cabbie obligingly double-parked. "That's three sixty-five for the fare and five dollars for the mess," he demanded.

"That's highway robbery." Marcus addressed the remark to Ann before he extracted a ten-dollar bill from his wallet and handed it to the man. "But even at that, it cost less than buying off the waitress. That little episode cost me a twenty-dollar tip."

Ann grimaced in acknowledgment of his thrust. "I'm perfectly willing to admit that the twenty to the waitress was my fault. I should never have let the mouse out of my purse. I'll pay you back," she promised rashly.

"You keep mice in your purse, lady?" the cabbie glanced apprehensively at her.

"Of course not. Only one mouse."

"Oh, that makes it all right." the man said with heavy irony. "As long as he doesn't have any friends."

Ann barely heard him; she was too taken up with trying to decide what to do. Was she supposed to get out? Stay where she was? Fortunately, Marcus solved her problem for her.

"Out," he ordered.

She obediently scooted out of the cab, waiting on the sidewalk as Marcus slammed the door behind them. The cabbie, apparently only too eager to escape, pulled away.

Marcus ran his hand down over his lean hip and then snorted in disgust. His fingers were covered with whipped cream and bits of strawberries.

Sweet strawberries overlying salty skin... the erotic thought flooded Ann's tired mind, to be followed by images of Marcus's tanned body covered with the plump, juicy berries. Images of her eating them off his strong, muscular chest. Of her pink tongue licking sensuously over his supple skin. Of her lips burrowing through a cloud of whipped cream to kiss the column of his strong brown neck. A quiver shook her, and she felt the muscles of her abdomen involuntarily clench.

You're out of your feeble little mind, she admonished herself. Standing in front of a strange house, in a strange neighborhood, with an equally strange man, who very shortly was going to demand to know why she absconded with a mouse from his lab, and instead of being worried about the situation she was indulging in a sexual fantasy.

"Ah!" His satisfied expression caught her attention and she turned, only too eager to avoid examining her uncharacteristic reaction to him.

"I found the key," he explained, ushering her up the half flight of broad stone steps to the house's black enameled front door. Long narrow windows were set in the stone on both sides of the entrance, and a gorgeous antique fanlight topped it.

Marcus inserted the key and unlocked the door. He pushed it open and reached inside, flipping on a switch.

Ann blinked in the sudden light as she allowed him to nudge her inside and close the door behind them. Curiously, she looked around. It appeared he was in the middle of renovating the interior. Several walls had been framed out, piles of building materials were scattered about and a stack of interior doors were propped up against one of the house's outside walls. A raw, gaping hole in the wall behind her was evidence that a fireplace had once been there. She walked over to the opening, wondering if he planned on replacing it. She frowned having noticed a thick carpet of dust on the hearth. For some reason, work seemed to have come to a halt.

"Are you remodeling?"

"I was." He gestured her up the ornately carved oak staircase to her left, but she pretended not to notice.

"What happened? Did you run out of money?" she asked sympathetically.

"No, patience. I bought this place three years ago as an investment. It was an excellent buy, and I thought it would be easy enough to remodel. What I didn't take into account was how distracting all the construction would be. It was impossible for me to get any work done at home. But the final straw came when when one of the carpenters took a critical lab report off my desk to use for scrap paper. That was when I told them to clear out."

"Oh?" Ann said, not understanding how anyone could simply ignore this mess. It would drive her out of her mind within a week. "But you've been in California for a year. Why didn't you have it finished then?"

"I meant to." He shook his hand, and she watched as globs of smashed berries landed on the dust-covered floor. "But with one thing and another, I forgot about it."

He'd forgotten? She stared at him in disbelief. He had simply locked his door and gone off to California without even remembering that his house looked like a storage shed for a construction firm. Try as she might, Ann simply couldn't relate to a list of priorities in which a wonderful old place like this was forgotten for the better part of a year. It made her wonder about Marcus, about what else he was liable to forget. He'd been married, she remembered Gladys's words. Maybe he had forgotten about his ex-wife, too, only to wake up one morning and find himself divorced.

"If you're through admiring the mementos of the construction crew, do you suppose we could find that nemesis in white fur a cage?" Marcus demanded, motioning toward the stairs.

"Certainly." Ann hurried to ascend. So that was why he'd brought her home. To find a cage for Serendipity, not because he wanted to seduce her. But strangely enough, this information, instead of calming her, merely depressed her. Just once she'd have liked to have been swept off her feet by a man. Reminding herself that she wasn't the type, she buried her vague longings beneath her practical exterior and decided to make the best of the situation. At least she was going to get a cage for Serendipity.

As she skirted the second-floor landing, she peered into the gloom. What little the shadows revealed seemed to be simply more of what was downstairs.

However, the third floor proved to be different. As she stepped onto the landing, the lights came on and she jumped in surprise.

"How did you do that!" she demanded.

"I didn't. You crossed an electronic beam that activated the lights."

"A light switch would accomplish the same thing without the shock to your visitor's nerves," she said dryly, looking around her in interest.

The front of the third floor was one huge room. The dark oak bookcases lining two of the walls were crammed to overflowing with books, magazines, folders and index cards. Everywhere they'd spilled off shelves to litter the honey-beige wall-to-wall carpeting. A brown leather sofa had been pulled away from a wall, as if someone had moved it and then forgotten to replace it. An overstuffed chair was sitting in the middle of the room, the empty box in front of it evidently serving as a footrest and the stack of dark green books beside it as an end table to hold a reading lamp.

Sitting in front of the triple windows that faced the street was the biggest desk Ann had ever seen. Every inch of its surface was cluttered with an incredible litter of papers, magazines, lab equipment and what seemed to her eyes to be plain junk. She wrinkled her nose fastidiously and reached out to remove a brown banana peel.

"Don't touch anything on that desk!" Marcus ordered. "I know exactly where everything is."

"Exactly what is everything?" She waved a hand over it.

"Lab reports, letters, that kind of thing."

"What you need is a secretary." *Or a computer*, she thought, her eyes narrowing.

"I had one," he shuddered. "In two days that woman managed to lose a paper I was supposed to present, the notes from an experiment and a requisition form for some equipment it had taken me the better part of a year to talk the director into signing."

Marcus's information-processing dilemma fled Ann's mind when he casually began to strip off his knit shirt. She watched the well-developed muscles of his biceps bulge as he wadded his shirt into a ball and tossed it in the general direction of the sofa.

With a primitive interest seemingly totally divorced from her normal, rational self, her eyes traced the prominent line of his left collarbone to the deep vee at the base of his neck and out across his other shoulder. Her eyelids half-closed and breathing in a strange rhythm, she swung her gaze back to his bare chest. A heavy coating of black hair curled over the flat planes of his chest and arrowed downward to disappear beneath his pants—pants he was busily removing.

"What do you think you're doing?" She winced at the tone of her words. She sounded like some impossibly prim spinster. "I mean . . ." She cleared her throat and tried again. "If you take your pants off in here, you'll get mashed strawberries on the carpet."

Marcus glanced down at the dusty floor. "Does it matter?"

"Yes," she insisted.

"Okay. Come on." He opened the room's one door. "I'll get the cage for the mouse."

Ann followed along in his wake, curious to see the rest of the floor. A huge bed had been shoved against one wall, and she stared at it in surprise. It was a hideous example of early Gothic. Elaborately carved grinning gargoyles decorated the platform, the posts and the wooden canopy frame.

Marcus noticed her expression. "You get used to it."

"You, maybe, but not me," she stated with utter conviction. "Where on earth did you find it?"

"The previous owners left it when they moved."

"That I can understand." Looking around to see what else they'd left—apparently nothing—she studied the barren room. It's very impersonality was chilling. One nightstand beside the bed and a plain chest of drawers against the opposite wall were the room's only other furniture, although stacks of books and magazines littered the floor in here, too.

"I think . . ." Marcus muttered, opening the door to what was obviously a closet and beginning to rummage around inside. Two innocuous-looking ties, one dark green and one pale blue, came flying out to be followed seconds later by his triumphant shout.

"I knew I had one around here somewhere." He emerged from the closet holding a lab cage. "Here." He handed it to her. "Dust it off while I take a shower."

"While you take a shower?"

"Absolutely. This stuff is sticky, and I refuse to take you home dripping strawberries. Now get that cleaned up. I won't be ten minutes."

"Sure." She tried to act as if sitting in a man's bedroom while he took a shower was an everyday occurrence. After all, she wasn't some shy, young thing who didn't have a clue. She was a shy, old thing, who'd been married for seven years, and still didn't have a clue. At least according to her ex-husband.

"What'll I use to clean it?" she called after him.

"Use that yellow shirt I just took off. It's dirty anyway." He disappeared into the bathroom.

"Men!" Ann grimaced, ignoring his suggestion. Instead she used a box of Kleenex she found on a stack of books beside the bed. Once she was satisfied that it was clean, she rescued Serendipity from her purse and popped him into the cage.

"There. Is that better, you poor little thing?" She sat down on the bed beside him. Serendipity, after one affronted glare, retreated to the far side of the cage, curled up in a ball and promptly went to sleep.

"An excellent idea," Ann said around a yawn. "It's a good thing I can sleep late tomorrow because by the time I get home it's going to be so late, it'll be early." She yawned again, fatigue washing over her in waves. When Marcus had left, he seemed to have taken her small store of energy with him.

Wearily, she lay back, allowing her body to sink into the surprisingly firm mattress. She'd just close her eyes for a minute, and when she heard the shower stop running she'd sit up again and figure out how she was going to explain Serendipity to Marcus.

3

THE MUTED SOUNDS of the Saturday-morning traffic from the city street below penetrated Ann's sleep. With a nasty mutter at the unwelcome intrusion, she buried her head deeper into the down pillow, sighing contentedly as its thick softness cushioned the movement. The very faint aroma of a masculine cologne prodded her drowsy senses.

"Hmmm." She wiggled sensuously beneath the thick satin comforter as the tangy scent of lime registered in her drowsy mind. It smelled so good. So essentially masculine. Her eyes flew open, and she found herself staring straight into the protuberant eyes of a gargoyle, who was leering obscenely at her. She blinked and looked again, but the apparition didn't obligingly vanish. As a matter of fact, the thing had been joined by its friends, a whole bedpost of monstrosities.

Bedpost? She frowned, propping herself up on her elbow and looking around in confusion. A confusion that was quickly laid to rest as memory came flooding back. She was in Marcus's bedroom, more specifically in his bed.

She remembered Marcus had gone to take a shower, and she'd lain down on his bed to wait . . . and fallen asleep. She groaned in disgust at her lack of self-control. Not only had she gone to sleep, but she had stayed there. Looking at the clock, she saw with dismay that it was ten-thirty in the morning. Ann flipped back the comforter and grimaced at the rumpled state of her jeans and thin knit shirt.

She thought of Marcus then, and her gaze automatically swung to the other side of the huge bed. Undoubtedly he had shared it with her last night. Somehow she couldn't picture pragmatic Marcus spending the night huddled on the sofa when there was a half-empty bed in the next room. Especially considering the fact that it was his house and his bed.

Her speculation came to an abrupt halt when she noticed the folded piece of paper with her name on it, lying amidst the litter on the bedside table. Gingerly she picked it up, smoothing it open. Heavy black strokes leaped out at her. Her eyes dropped to the signature, noting the boldly scrawled Marcus. Of course it was from Marcus, she thought in self-derision. There was no one else here except Serendipity.

A nervous giggle escaped her to echo eerily in the bare room. Unless the institute had been fooling around with radiation, the chance of Serendipity having written anything were nil. Determinedly she banished the fatuous thought and read the note. The handwriting was surprisingly clear and the words discouragingly brief. They stated that he'd gone to the lab and would get in touch with her later.

Sure he would. Her lips twisted in a wry grimace as she remembered the fiasco of their one date. A fiasco she'd topped off by falling asleep and spending the night uninvited. There was no way he was ever going to call her again. Not that she wanted him to, she told herself. Her life was already full to overflowing with her job, school and studying. She didn't have any time for distractions right now, and Marcus most definitely was a distraction. She climbed out of bed, stretched and yawned.

At least she'd been spared having to face him this morning, she reflected, trying to look on the bright side. Her

limited social experience hadn't provided her with a prec-
edent for handling this kind of situation, and the article
she'd read on modern dating practices wasn't proving to be
much help. The examples the author had used had all been
ordinary dates. From start to finish, there had been nothing ordinary about her brief association with Marcus. In-
cluding the way he'd left her to sleep and gone off to work.

A horrible thought suddenly occurred to her. Marcus had
gone back to the lab, and he might well have taken Serendipity with him. She glanced around the bedroom. It's bar-
renness made a thorough search unnecessary. There was no
mouse to be seen. She rushed into the front room, but there
was no silver cage amidst the litter on the desk. Or anywhere else for that matter.

She sagged against the doorframe, feeling as if she'd just
betrayed a friend. If only she'd been awake when Marcus
had left, he'd never have taken Serendipity with him. A
militant gleam lit her eyes before common sense doused it.
There had to be something she could do about his treach-
ery. She could hardly march over to the lab and demand her
mouse back, though. Marcus would simply ignore her,
provided he even remembered who she was, Ann amended,
remembering Gladys's warning.

She simply had to face it—she had lost and so had poor
Serendipity. She swallowed the lump in her throat, trying
to listen to the rational part of her mind telling her that,
when all was said and done, Serendipity was only a mouse.

Taking a deep breath, Ann straightened up and went back
into the bedroom, intending to wash her face before leaving. She walked into the bath, letting out a startled yelp
when the lights suddenly went on. Blast Marcus and his
electronic toys! She mentally consigned him to perdition.

"Serendipity!" She gasped at the sight of the silver bars
of his cage, a tiny pink nose pushing between them.

"Cherrup." His long whiskers twitched happily, and Ann laughed as a feeling of lighthearted relief swept over her.

Marcus wasn't a coldhearted scientist willing to sacrifice everything for his research after all. He'd left her her mouse. And something else. She cautiously opened the brown grocery sack propped up beside the cage; having seen his house, she knew it was liable to contain anything. What it did contain were several pounds of mouse food and another note. Eagerly she pulled it out, frowning slightly at the five-dollar bill stapled to the top.

"Take a cab home and don't overfeed him, too," she read. Too? Too what? A frown furrowed her brow as she tried to figure out what he'd meant, but nothing immediately occurred to her. Since she knew almost nothing about Marcus's thought processes, it would have to remain a mystery, although she was certain there was an insult buried there somewhere.

As for the money. . . Ann thoughtfully fingered the crisp bill. Her initial impulse was to leave it behind in a prominent spot, but she thought better of the idea almost immediately. It was all well and good to be independent, but there was a difference between pride and obstinacy. Marcus was, after all, merely providing her with transportation home after a date. If she hadn't been so stupid as to have fallen asleep last night, he'd have taken her home in a taxi and she wouldn't have thought a thing about it. So what was the difference in his paying for the cab this morning?

None, she concluded. In fact he might consider it well worth the five dollars to get rid of her and her mouse. The thought depressed her, and she hastily pushed it to the back of her mind. If that was what he wanted, she'd take his money. She stuffed the bill into her pants pocket. Besides, she reminded herself, if she didn't take it, she was going to have a long walk home because they'd never let her on the bus carrying a mouse.

"Cherrup." Serendipity's aggrieved squeak cut into her thoughts.

"Hungry, handsome?" Ann softly stroked his tiny head. "You'll have to wait until we get home." Her stomach growled at the thought of food, and she sighed regretfully at the fate of her strawberry pie.

She flipped on the crystal faucet in one of the twin sinks and splashed cold water over her face. Then dried it off with the thick yellow towel that had been dropped on the vanity top. She hung it neatly over the towel rack.

Curiously she looked around the oversize bathroom, noting the separate shower compartment, the beautiful metallic wallpaper and the double sink with its marbled top. Her gaze came to rest longingly on the huge raised tub to her left. It was easily six feet long and fitted with whirlpool jets. For a brief moment she weighed the idea of soaking in the swirling water. It had been over a year since she'd been able to indulge in a long, leisurely bath. The bathroom that she shared with the other three tenants on her floor contained only a shower.

Wistfully she turned her back on the temptation. It would be the last straw if Marcus returned to find her cavorting in his tub. Or if he simply returned and found her. Period. The thought prodded her into action. She grabbed Serendipity's cage in one hand and picked up the sack of food in the other. Marcus's patience couldn't be expected to last forever. He'd been very forebearing about her stealing the mouse. Surprisingly forbearing. Granted, he'd been angry about the restaurant incident, but his fury hadn't lasted. And when he'd had the perfect opportunity to exact revenge for what she'd put him through last night by taking

Serendipity back to the lab, he hadn't. Instead he'd provided food for him. She couldn't imagine why.

Ann grimaced, speculating about Marcus's possible motives was useless as well as distracting. And she didn't need any distractions right now, she reminded herself once again.

Not that she didn't have time for pleasure, she involuntarily rebutted the sense of chill emptiness that filled her. This afternoon, after she'd dispensed with her normal Saturday chores, she was going to start the ancient dog-eared edition of *Nicomachean Ethics* she'd unearthed last Saturday in the dingy basement of her favorite bookstore. All week long, she'd been looking forward to reading the work in the original Greek, but somehow the treat seemed to have lost some of its original savor. Ann resolutely ignored that fact, picking up the phone on Marcus's desk to call a cab.

"THANK GOD this week is over." Gladys sank down onto a vinyl chair in the empty employee lounge, stretched her swollen ankles out in front of her and fanned her face with her hand. "I thought it would never end."

"Hmm," Ann murmured from the depths of her locker, echoing Gladys's sentiments. The week had seemed endless. Her FORTRAN teacher had suddenly turned into Attila the Hun, assigning tons of homework; the weather had been stiflingly hot, giving her unair-conditioned efficiency all the attractions of Dante's inferno. And always, buried in the back of her mind, was the vague hope that Marcus had really meant it when he'd said he'd be in touch. But, finally, after a whole week of silence, she was forced to admit that her initial conclusion had been correct. It had been a polite meaningless phrase, the kind long used by men to gently sever relationships.

Not that they'd had a relationship. They were barely more than casual acquaintances, despite having spent the night together.

"You got a date with Marvelous Marcus?" Gladys's question uncannily meshed with Ann's thoughts.

"Nope." Ann ran a comb through her tousled hair.

"Too bad," Gladys sighed.

"Yup, it was a great meal." She squinted at her reflection in the tiny mirror on the inside of her locker door.

"Food!" Gladys snorted. "Who cares about food at your age. What about Marvelous Marcus? Is he as great as they say?" Her eyes gleamed with friendly curiosity.

"He was very—" Ann reached for a word and finally settled on "—forbearing."

"Forbearing!" Gladys's mouth fell open. "If you don't want to tell me, just say so."

"I don't want to tell you," Ann repeated with a laugh. "Not that there's anything to tell. He bought me a meal and took me home," she offered, giving an expurgated version of last Friday's events.

"Well—" Gladys heaved a sigh "—it's probably for the best anyway. What you need is a nice steady man with a normal job. Someone like my cousin Mavis's boy."

"That's what I like about you, Gladys, you're so subtle."

"Being subtle never got a girl a husband."

No, but being stupid would, Ann thought acidly, remembering her own marriage. In the interests of peace, however, she kept the thought to herself.

"I do have a date tomorrow night, though."

"But I thought you said that he . . ."

"Not with Marcus, with Nicomachus."

"Nicom . . ."

"Nicomachus, Aristotle's son."

"Oh, is he that Greek butcher down the street?"

"He only butchers words." Ann's eyes danced with laughter. "He's a philosopher."

"A philosopher!" Gladys rolled her eyes in disgust. "My cousin's boy's a welder. That'll put food on the table."

"I don't need food. We got paid on Tuesday, remember?"

"Ha! We get so little it's easy enough to forget."

"Ain't it the truth," Ann paraphrased as she gathered up her purse. "Have a nice weekend."

"You, too." Gladys reluctantly abandoned her matchmaking. "Watch where you're going." she called after Ann.

"I will," she called back truthfully. She'd spent the past week very carefully watching where she was going. Half hoping, half fearing that she would catch a glimpse of Marcus in the institute's hallways. But she hadn't. He'd remained an elusive figure, making her wonder if, perhaps, he was out of town. She knew she could always ask Gladys. What Gladys didn't know about the movements of the institute's staff wasn't worth knowing. But Ann was reluctant to admit the extent of her interest in him even to herself, let alone to her garrulous friend.

"DON'T LOOK AT ME like that. I have no intention of spending my Saturday afternoon mouse-sitting."

"Cherrup." Serendipity wiggled his pink nose, obviously protesting.

"You've got lots of food and plenty of fresh water. You'll be fine. However, I'm not so sure about you, Ann Somerton. Talking to a mouse as if he could understand every word you said." She shook her head ruefully and, picking up her purse, let herself out of her tiny efficiency, making certain that the lock had caught behind her. Not that she had anything worth stealing, but break-ins were rife in the neighborhood, and she had no desire to walk in on a burglar.

She carefully made her way down the steep steps to the first floor, blinking as she emerged into the brilliant July sunshine. She slipped her purse strap over her shoulder and started down the concrete steps to the sidewalk, almost falling when she heard Marcus's voice from the side of the stoop.

"It's lunchtime."

Ann swung around as if tethered by his dark velvet voice and stared at him in surprise. Compulsively her gaze skimmed over his broad forehead, slid down his faintly crooked nose and slipped past his square chin to measure the intimidating breadth of his heavily muscled chest, which was covered by a blue knit shirt. As she remembered the sight of those muscles rippling under his tanned skin, her eyes narrowed slightly. She moistened her lower lip and tightened her grip on her purse, her fingertips tingling at the memory of the pelt of crisp black hair covering that broad chest. She swallowed, unnerved by her reaction to him. It made no sense. She'd always thought of herself as an intellectual person rather than a sensual one. Determinedly she forced herself to meet his bright blue eyes.

"Still haven't figured out the dynamics of conversation, I see," she remarked, not entirely successful in banishing the pleasure she felt at seeing him from her voice.

"Hello, dear lady." He straightened up and moved toward her. "It's lunchtime."

"Good afternoon. Yes, I know." She braced herself against the feel of his long fingers closing over her upper arm. A burning warmth that had nothing to do with the July heat branded her skin, and tiny sparks of awareness flashed along her nerve endings. "What are you doing?" she asked when he began to hustle her down the steps.

"Taking you to lunch, of course."

"Lunch?" she echoed. Visions of the last time she'd been in a restaurant with him rose to haunt her. She doubted that she'd ever be that hungry for a meal again.

"No, thanks." She determinedly dug in her heels and came to a halt on the sidewalk. "I have other plans."

"All right, we'll do what you want." Marcus hastily side-stepped a girl on a skateboard, pulling Ann against his chest as he did so. She shivered at the sensation of the hard length of him imprinting itself on her much softer flesh.

"Honestly," she muttered, "between the muggers, the kids and the dogs, the sidewalks aren't safe anymore."

"Oh, I don't know." His eyes twinkled down at her, and he gave her a slight squeeze. "The situation is not without its compensations. Now then—" he released her and stepped back "—where are we going?"

She gave up. "To the bookstore first." Her intellect might know that Marcus represented a threat to her hard-won peace of mind, but her emotions seemed unable to resist the pull he was exerting. It couldn't hurt to go out with him in broad daylight, she assured herself without any real conviction.

"Then we stop at a restaurant?" he asked hopefully.

"No, then I'm going to a friend's house for lunch."

"I'll come, too." He smiled happily at her, and an answering smile curved her lips at the unabashed way he invited himself along. Apparently conversation wasn't the only area of his social expertise that had been neglected.

"All right," she agreed, wondering how the afternoon would turn out. Peggy was always telling her to bring a date along, but somehow Ann didn't think that Marcus was quite what she had in mind.

Peggy and Tom Walker were the only friends Ann had left from her married days. They'd helped her to cope with the emotional turmoil of her divorce. In truth, Ann no longer

had anything in common with them but shared memories.
She was fiercely loyal to them, though, and had no intention of apologizing to anyone for their complete lack of interest in anything even vaguely approaching the intellectual.
Tom worked in a factory and spent all of his free time in
front of the television set, while Peggy helped out part-time
in a fabric store and coped with the rigors of raising three
growing boys.

"Where is this bookstore?" inquired Marcus, interrupt-
ing her worries; she allowed them to melt away.

"Over on Thirty-fourth Street just past the Empire State
Building. About fifteen blocks away." She eyed him uncertainly. There wasn't an ounce of fat on him, but that didn't
mean he was physically fit. "We could take a bus. Or your
car?" She suddenly wondered how he'd gotten there.

"I don't have one. We'll walk." He matched his words to
action.

"You don't have a car?" she repeated in astounded tones.
Everyone she knew either owned one or wished they did.
Herself included. She hated sprinting for buses that were
early or getting drenched while waiting in the rain for ones
that were late.

"I did. Years ago," he admitted, "but it wasn't to be
trusted."

"Not to be trusted?" she repeated, frowning. "You mean
you had a driver?"

"No, the car wasn't to be trusted. It never worked.
Something was always going wrong or else it was out of gas.
Machines aren't to be trusted," he reiterated.

"On what level?"

"Any level." He paused in front of a deli and began to read
the menu stuck in the window.

"That's ridiculous!"

"I'll say. They don't have any bagels."

"No, I meant your attitude toward machines. Machines are simply tools designed to help man cope with his environment."

"No they aren't." Marcus pulled her into the deli. "They're inventions of the devil specifically designed to drive man crazy."

"They don't drive me crazy."

"You aren't a man." He gave her a smug smile.

"And you're being totally illogical." Ann found the knowledge strangely comforting. He might be a world-renowned biochemist, but he wasn't perfect.

"Realistic," he insisted. "Would you like anything?" He motioned toward the glass cabinet that held a mouth-watering assortment of pastries. "I'm going to have a sub. Everything on it and heavy on the hot peppers." Marcus instructed the elderly clerk behind the counter.

"Where are you going to eat that?" She glanced around the tiny shop. "There aren't any chairs."

"I'll eat it while we're walking to the bookstore."

"You can't walk down the street eating a sandwich!"

"A sub", he corrected.

"It's the same thing."

"Only if you don't have any taste buds."

"Don't be dense!" she admonished, and then gave a weak smile to the old man who was openly staring at her.

"And you said I was illogical," Marcus complained. "I'm hungry and there's no place to sit in here, so why shouldn't I eat it while we walk?"

"Because it's bad manners."

"Don't be so parochial, and I'll share with you."

Ann watched him pay for the food, and she considered his charge. Was she parochial simply because she felt it was bad manners to walk down the street eating a sandwich?

She followed Marcus out of the deli, watching enviously as he sank his strong white teeth into the thick sub. It looked delicious.

Marcus shot her a penetrating glance and asked, "Why?"

"Why what?"

"Why is it bad manners to eat while walking down the street?"

"Well . . ." Ann struggled for words. "My mother always said . . ." She trailed off uncertainly. Her mother had said lots of things, among them that marriage to Steve was a good idea.

"Want a bite?" He held out his sub.

Ann looked at the succulent layers of meat and cheese topped with lettuce, tomatoes, peppers and vinegar.

"Sure," she declared recklessly. She took a bite of the sandwich, feeling as if she'd just made an important discovery. Marcus was right. It didn't matter. They didn't raise a flicker of interest in the passersby. No one cared in the slightest. Happily, she matched her stride to his, and they made their way to the bookstore.

"This is a bookstore?" Marcus looked disbelievingly around the dimly lit interior.

"It's a used bookstore," she explained.

"Used? But that means that all the books are outdated."

"What do you mean outdated?"

"That the information contained in these books—" he gestured toward the crowded shelves "—is out of date. It's been superseded by more recent findings. So why would you bother to read it?"

"Well, that's true enough for some types of books," she conceded. "But fiction is fiction, and of course the classics don't change."

"I don't read fiction. Only scientific reports."

"And you had the nerve to call me parochial!"

"Fiction is a waste of time."

"But what do you read for entertainment? Or do you watch television?" Ann recalled Steve's fascination with the media.

"I don't have a television, and I told you that I read scientific reports."

"Hmm." She eyed him narrowly, rather disconcerted by his attitude. "You, sir, have the makings of a first-class intellectual snob."

"I do not!" he insisted. "I read what I'm interested in."

"But surely you must have some interest besides cancer research?"

"I find you interesting." His eyes took on a wicked gleam.

"I was referring to books." She beat down the feeling of excitement his words raised. "When was the last time you read any fiction."

"My sophomore year of college in a required English course. We read *Madame Bovary* and *As I Lay Dying*."

"Faulkner," Ann mused.

"Damnedest thing I ever read. Can you imagine any woman being stupid enough to think that since having sex had gotten her pregnant, having sex again would cause an abortion?"

Ann winced, having heard smothered laughter from the college-aged boy behind the cash register to their right.

"And those bananas!" Marcus recalled another grievance from the book. "And not only that, but do you have any idea what a body would smell like after having been jolted around in an open wagon through the back roads of the Deep South in the heat of the summer!"

"That's disgusting!"

"I'll say it would be," he agreed.

"I meant . . ." Ann paused, realizing that he was never going to appreciate the book's symbolism. "Perhaps Faulkner's an acquired taste," she soothed. "But surely you couldn't have disliked *Madame Bovary*!"

"I couldn't find the third angel."

"Huh?"

"Our literature professor said that there were three angels in the book. One at each turning point in her life. I found the one on her wedding cake when she married that poor sucker and the one carved in the mantel when she had her first affair, but I couldn't find the third one."

Ann opened her mouth, closed it again and simply stared at him. "You have a very good memory," she finally said.

"Of course I do. It goes with my job."

"You've also set the field of literature back a hundred years. It's a disgrace that a man of your intellectual capabilities doesn't read."

"I do too read! I read all the time."

"Reading reports doesn't qualify. That's just scientific mumbo-jumbo."

"Having been exposed to your thought processes, I can understand why you find them incomprehensible," he shot back.

"We're going to have to develop a reading program for you. There has to be something you like."

"I told you—"

"No, I meant real literature," Ann interrupted.

"And you called me an intellectual snob!"

"Never mind, we'll find something for you."

"Why did we come in here?" Marcus asked.

"Because it's the first Saturday after payday."

"So?"

"So that's the day I treat myself to a couple of used books. Last time I was here I found a copy of *Nicomachian Ethics* in the original Greek." Ann started toward the back steps that lead to the basement.

"If Aristotle had paid a little more attention to his family, he'd have found that kid a decent job, and the world would have been spared one more infernal philosopher."

His attitude would have done credit to Gladys. Ann swallowed a grin at the thought. She flipped on the light switch in the stairwell, sighing in resignation when nothing happened.

"Hold on to the railing," she warned. "The stairs are steep."

"Why don't we look at the books up here. At least we can see the titles."

"It's not that bad." They rounded the bend at the bottom of the stairs and emerged into the dimly lit basement. There were several people shifting through the boxes of books covering the floor. "And this is where the real bargains are to be found. The store buys out entire estates and dumps them down here." She squatted beside the nearest box and began to search methodically through it.

"What are we looking for?" Marcus asked in resignation.

"Anything in either Latin or Greek or something that you think looks interesting." She ignored his incredulous look. "If you don't find anything for yourself down here, we'll check the shelves upstairs."

"Threats will get you nowhere," Marcus muttered.

ANN STOOD UP and stretched, absently rubbing her dusty fingers over her jeans-clad hips. She wriggled her stiff shoulders and glanced around, frowning when she realized that Marcus was no longer burrowing through the boxes on the other side of the basement. He'd disappeared while she'd been skimming through the copy of *Phaedo* she'd found.

A frisson of disappointment shivered through her at the thought that he might have simply left. He was turning out to be surprisingly good company. Perhaps he was exploring the rest of the store, she decided hopefully.

Picking up the book she'd selected, she went upstairs. Marcus wasn't in the large front room, so she headed toward the smaller rooms in the back, which were given over to genre fiction. She didn't really expect him to be there, considering his opinion of fiction, but her only alternative was to ask the young man behind the cash register if Marcus had left. Her pride wouldn't allow her to admit that she'd misplaced her escort, so that was out of the question.

He wasn't in either of the next two rooms she checked. Going all the way to the back seemed a waste of time since there were only romance books in that area, but it was either that or admit that he wasn't in the store so she did.

To her surprise, she found him alone in the room, seated on a box of unpacked books, studying a thick paperback. Fascinated, she watched the expressions chasing over his face. First, one side of his sensual mouth quirked upward in what she thought was a sneer, but could have been indigestion. Then his eyebrows made a bid to escape into his thick black hair. His forehead furrowed in concentration as he wiggled his eyebrows again. Finally, unable to contain her curiosity, she walked over to him.

"Marcus, what are you doing?"

"Oh, there you are." He moved over to the edge of the box and Ann, accepting the unspoken invitation, sank down beside him. Her slim thigh was pressed against the hard length of his muscular one, and a shiver chased over her skin as the heat from his leg penetrated her jeans. She licked her lips nervously, but refused to move. She might not understand her body's reaction to Marcus, but she certainly didn't fear it. At least, not exactly. Taking a deep breath, she tried to block out her response.

"You didn't tell me what you were doing."

"A cynical sneer followed by an attempt to sardonically arch one mobile eyebrow."

"What?" She stared blankly at him.

"A cynical sneer," he repeated absently as he flipped another page, "but I'm not sure about the mobile eyebrow."

"I'm not so sure about you." She eyed him warily. "What on earth are you talking about?"

"I'm looking into fiction."

"Romantic fiction!"

"I decided to start at the back of the store, and this is what was here," he explained.

"Somehow, I can't see you reading romantic fiction."

"Well . . ." He seemed to give her words careful consideration. "It's certainly no worse than dragging a body around Mississippi."

"Will you forget about that body!"

"Gladly. You were the one who brought it up in the first place."

"And I'm beginning to regret it," she muttered. "Exactly what is it that you're reading?" She reached for the book, but he held it away.

"Go find your own. This one's just getting interesting. The hero, or villain—I'm not sure which he is—finally gave up arching his mobile eyebrow and is now ripping the 'thin chemise from her generous bosom,'" he replied, reading on. "Now that's an interesting concept." His eyes gleamed with devilry. "I wonder who they were generous to?" His gaze dropped to Ann's small breasts, clearly outlined under her thin cotton shirt.

She felt a fugitive heat warm her cheeks and lunged for the book. Unfortunately, his reflexes were more than equal to the occasion, and he whipped it out of her reach. She lost her balance and landed sprawled across his hard thighs.

"Now you're getting into the spirit of things," he approved. "It's too bad you haven't got a chemise for me to rip off."

"Well, you can't arch your eyebrow, either!" she snapped, groaning inwardly at the idiocy of the remark.

"True," he agreed. "I guess I'll have to give up all aspirations to be a pirate."

"Oh, I don't know," Ann muttered, trying to squirm off his lap. She paused when it suddenly struck her that his supposedly helping hands were turning her more fully into him.

"What are you doing?" She put her fingers on his chest and tentatively pushed, but he didn't budge and neither did her fingers. Their tips seemed glued to the warm knit of his pale blue shirt. She could feel the springy texture of his chest hair and underneath that the beat of his heart; the steady, rhythmic beat of his heart.

"Trying to give the book a fair chance. Maybe holding a beautiful woman helps with the sardonic drawl." He grinned down at her.

Her eyes lingered on the deep cleft in his chin, and she savored his offhand compliment, finding it unexpectedly sweet. All the more so because she knew it wasn't true. At her best she could be classified as attractive, never beautiful.

"But you aren't doing your part." Marcus raised his arm to consult the book and in the process managed to squash her into his chest.

Ann swallowed convulsively as the tangy aroma of his after-shave drifted into her lungs.

"Ah, here we are." He loosened his grip slightly, and she forced her head back.

"You're supposed to lift your chin, glare at me from glorious—" the last word rolled off his tongue and landed in the pit of her stomach, where it raised all kinds of havoc "—turquoise eyes." He paused and peered down into her plain brown ones. "No matter," he decreed, "we'll make the best of it."

Or the most of it. She took shorter breaths, hoping to block out the insidious aroma of his after-shave. She didn't. All she managed to do was make herself even more aware of the clean underlying smell of the man himself.

"And spit."

"Spit?" The word penetrated the sensual fog that was closing down the rational part of her mind. "How unsanitary."

"Never, you bastard."

"What!" Her eyes flew open at the insult.

"Not you. You're supposed to spit, 'Never, you bastard!' And I'm supposed to drawl, 'Never is a long time.'"

"And getting longer by the minute." Her outraged features relaxed. "Marcus, these books aren't realistic. They're simply sexual fantasies."

"Being ravished by a strange pirate with a mobile eyebrow?" He looked astonished.

"I didn't say they were mine!" she snapped.

"What kind of sexual fantasies do you have?" His softly whispered words grated over her skin, raising goose bumps as they went. "Being ravished in a bookstore?"

"This is not at all a proper subject for discussion," she said primly. "And, besides, I'm not into ravishments."

"Just as well." He nodded decisively. "Ravishing someone sounds painful."

"Painful?" she replied weakly.

"Umm, according to this she tried to gouge his eyes out and then she 'raked red furrows down his lean brown flanks.'"

"Marcus, do you know that you are ruining entire fields of literature for me. You aren't supposed to take these things seriously."

"Gouging out eyes isn't serious?" He looked confused. "What else happens in the book?"

"I don't know and, quite frankly, I don't care," she said in exasperation.

"Actually," he mused, "writing books based on sexual fantasies isn't such a bad idea. I've always dreamed about kissing a gorgeous girl in the back room of a run-down bookstore. First, I gather her soft, pliant body into mine, and then I look deep into her eyes...."

"This is beginning to take on Draculaean overtones," she whispered, mesmerized by the tiny leaping lights in his bright blue eyes.

"Why on earth would anyone settle for a neck, even an elegant one like yours, when they could have your exquisite lips."

"Oh?" She blinked and made a bid to regain control of a situation that was fast slipping through her fingers. "Marcus, we're in a bookstore."

"You weren't listening. That's part of the fantasy, and this is the rest of it." He suddenly swooped, capturing her lips.

Ann's startled gasp was swallowed up by his warm mouth, and her eyes instinctively slid shut as a tingling sensation spread from the point of contact. The tip of his tongue outlined her clenched teeth, and startled by his action, her mouth opened, allowing his tongue to plunge inside.

A soft yearning sound began in the back of her throat and she pressed closer to him, trembling as her cheek scraped over his hair-roughened chin. The sensation was unbearably erotic and her trembling increased. To her dismay, Marcus suddenly lifted his head and set her back onto the box beside him.

Feeling bereft at the sudden loss of his lips, she took a deep breath and simultaneously became aware of two things. First, that Marcus hadn't severed all contact. His large hand was resting comfortingly on the small of her back. Second, and more important, the sound of footsteps was echoing in the hallway. Blindly, she reached for a book from the shelf in front of her, pretending to peruse the dust jacket while she hastily tried to control her rioting emotions. It made no sense. She'd been kissed hundreds of times. Thousands. She'd been married for almost eight years. But never before had she felt the turbulent sensations her body had just experienced or lost her sense of time and place.

Lord, she thought distractedly. If a simple kiss had done that to her nervous system, then what would happen if he made love to her? She immediately banished the thought. That was not the way to regain control of her emotions.

Ann glanced up as two women came into the room and headed for the Regencies under the window. It was time to leave, she told herself, and matching thought to action, she haphazardly replaced the book she was holding and stood up, vaguely surprised to find that her legs would support her.

"Where are we going?" Marcus asked. His matter-of-fact tones helped to steady her. He wasn't acting as if he'd just discovered what kissing was all about. He probably got the same reaction from all the women he kissed. The sobering thought stiffened her resolve.

"Out of here."

"All right." He obligingly stood up. "Fiction isn't really my thing."

"Fiction is everyone's thing," she insisted. "All we have to do is to find a type that appeals to you. The only thing we've actually established is that you don't like bodice rippers."

"And bodies being lugged around the South."

"You mention that body one more time, and it's going to have a companion!" Ann warned, and then winced when she noticed the avid expressions on the faces of the two women who had abandoned the book stacks in favor of frank eavesdropping.

"Come on, Marcus. I have an idea." She gave the women a nod and left, followed by Marcus.

"I shudder to ask, considering your past record, but what idea?"

"About what you should read." She frowned, peering into the tiny room to their right. "No, it's the next one. We'll start you out in science fiction."

"Science fiction!"

"Sure." She turned into the room that housed the science-fiction collection. "It's a natural. Lots of science-fiction writers are scientists. Asimov's a biochemist. At least, I think so," she qualified. "You'll love it."

"I already read what I love," he muttered.

"We'll start with a collection of short stories, I think." She selected a book at random. "That way you can sample lots of different authors."

"As long as we're sampling things . . ." His eyes began to gleam again and Ann, fearful of his habit of saying exactly what he was thinking, nudged him and pointed toward the elderly gentleman patiently sifting through the novellas.

"All right," Marcus accepted the book with a sigh, "I surrender. I'll read it."

"You'll love it," she repeated confidently. How could anyone fail to find at least one story he liked in a science-fiction anthology? She glanced down at her watch and whistled in surprise.

"We'd better hurry up, or we're going to be late for Peggy's. That is, if you still want to come?"

She waited for his answer, torn between an irrational desire for his company and the sure knowledge that getting involved with him was a bad idea. Not only was she much too busy, but she didn't want to get hurt when he lost interest and quit calling. And he would lose interest. She knew if he'd forgotten a gorgeous lab technician, with whom he could discuss his work, then he was certain to forget a nondescript classics scholar who doubled as a cleaning lady.

"Of course, I'm coming." He seemed surprised at her question, and Ann resolved to quit worrying and simply enjoy the novelty of having someone that she could talk to. Really talk to.

By the time the taxi had deposited them in front of Peggy and Tom's house in Queens, Ann was back to being nervous about how this luncheon was going to turn out. She couldn't imagine what Marcus would ever find to discuss with Tom. Tom's comsuming interest in life was watching sports on television, followed closely by watching anything else that was on. And with Marcus's nasty habit of saying exactly what he was thinking, it could be a very long afternoon.

Ann stepped over a bicycle lying across the cracked cement sidewalk leading to her friend's home, then paused.

"Marcus..." she began uncertainly. How did she ask him not to say anything that she was going to regret? She couldn't, she decided. Nor could she warn him about Peggy and Tom. What could she say? They aren't your intellectual equals? Who was? Besides, putting it into words not only sounded as if she was being patronizing toward her friends, but also that she thought Marcus was an intellectual snob. And despite her taunt earlier, she didn't think that.

"What?" He picked up the bike and dumped it on the small patch of hard-packed ground that was the front yard.

"Nothing," she sighed, and continued up the toy-strewn walk.

Peggy must have been watching their progress because the door swung open before they hit the top step of the porch. "Hi," she said, her gaze going beyond Ann to latch on to Marcus with avid curiosity.

"Hi, Peggy, I brought a friend with me." Ann stepped inside, followed by Marcus.

"Peggy, this is . . ." She stopped and frantically tried to decide how one should introduce a man who was both a Ph.D and an M.D. Doctor Blackmore? But that sounded so pretentious for what was really a social occasion. A real fun time, she thought wryly. "Marcus Blackmore," she said finally.

"Marcus, this is Peggy Walker."

"I'm so pleased to meet a friend of Ann's," Peggy gushed. "Come and meet my husband." She led the way into the living room.

Tom was sitting in a recliner, his attention focused on the blaring television. He looked up and smiled on seeing Ann, then turned the set down to a low roar.

"Come on in and rest your bones. Who's your friend?"

"Marcus Blackmore." Marcus introduced himself, shook Tom's outstretched hand and then sank down onto the threadbare sofa.

Ann glanced uncertainly at Marcus and sat down beside him with the vague intention of trying to divert potential problems.

"Glad to meet you," Tom said. "You're the first man Ann's brought by since—"

"Would you like some coffee?" Peggy hurriedly interrupted before Tom could mention Ann's divorce.

"No thanks." Marcus shook his head.

"Good choice," Tom laughed. "Peggy's one in a million, but she makes ghastly coffee. Do you work at the institute with Ann?"

"Yes," Marcus replied, nodding.

"Cleaning's all right for a woman, but it's no job for a man. My brother-in-law's shop's hiring. You got any experience with television repair?"

"No." Marcus shook his head. "I don't have one."

"Don't have—" Tom's mouth fell open, and he stared at Marcus with something akin to horror. "Everyone has a television."

"An inaccurate statement as I've just said I don't," Marcus observed. "Although I will admit that it sometimes seems that way. Especially at close range." He gave the still-blaring television a considering look, and Tom turned it down further.

"Good thing for my brother-in-law, or he'd be out of a job," Tom said, then laughed.

"Hmm." Marcus continued to watch for a few minutes longer and then turned to Ann. "Ravishment seems to be a universal theme. The only difference between the book I was looking at and this movie is that he's ripping off her sweater instead of a chemise. I wonder if he can arch one eyebrow?" he murmured.

"This is hardly literature," Ann said tightly. "It's... What is it?" she asked Tom.

"A movie I've got playing on the VCR. You saw a movie like this?" he asked Marcus curiously.

"No." Marcus continued to watch the action. "I never go to the movies."

"Me, neither," Tom replied. "I rent them from the video store down at the shopping center."

"Marcus just got back from California." Ann tried to steer the conversation along more innocuous lines.

"California!" Peggy breathed enviously. "I've always wanted to go, but it's so expensive to fly and Tom can never get away from the factory for longer than a week at a time. What did you think of Disneyland, Marcus?"

"I didn't go."

"Well, how about Hollywood?" Peggy persisted.

"No."

"Knott's Berry Farm? Grauman's Chinese Theater?" Peggy refused to give up.

"No," he replied simply.

"What did you do?"

"My work."

"But you couldn't have worked all the time."

"Quit badgering the guy, Peggy. Those places all cost a fortune, and he probably doesn't make that much as a janitor. You know," Tom went on, "you ought to do like Ann's doing and take a computer course. Like they say on television, you need a skill, if you want a job."

"I'd rather starve than work with computers!" Marcus stated emphatically.

A loud buzzing sound from the kitchen interrupted, and Peggy jumped to her feet. "Come on, Ann, the casserole's done. You can help me get lunch on the table."

"Certainly." She reluctantly got to her feet and followed Peggy out, not wanting to leave Marcus alone with Tom.

"Well?" Peggy demanded once they were safely in the kitchen. "Where did you find him?"

"I told you. At the institute." Ann perched on a stool at the breakfast bar and watched Peggy begin to shred lettuce.

"Are you serious about him?"

"Serious! Give me a break, Peggy. I only met the man last week."

"That's right. He said he'd just gotten back from California. Can you imagine being out there and not visiting anything?" Peggy was appalled.

"Well, actually I can. I couldn't care less about movie stars, and amusement parks leave me cold. I'd sure like to get inside Stanford University's library, though." Ann's eyes gleamed at the prospect.

"Maybe you and Marcus aren't as mismatched as I'd originally thought," Peggy said dryly.

"Insults will get you nowhere."

"It's just that he's so . . ." Peggy paused as if searching for words. "I'm not sure. Anyway, I can't see you with some guy who cleans labs for a living."

"He doesn't clean labs," Ann admitted. "As a matter of fact, he doesn't clean anything." She remembered the petrified banana peel on his desk.

"That's even worse! That he doesn't do what he's hired to do. And I'll bet you wind up doing a lot of his work. That's always been your trouble, Ann. You've got a soft heart."

"To go with my soft head, no doubt. Listen, Peggy, I don't pretend to understand why you continue to see me as some put-upon idiot who can't stand up for herself—"

"Because if you'd have had an ounce of gumption, you'd have ended your marriage six months after it began instead of letting it drag on for seven years. Seven long, wasted years."

"They were not wasted years," Ann insisted. "Anyway, that's all beside the point. What I'm trying to tell you is that Marcus is not a janitor. He's a biochemist who does cancer research. He also has an M.D. to his credit, although I don't think he's ever practiced."

"He's a what?" Peggy stared at Ann. "Then why did you say that he was a janitor?"

"I didn't!" Ann sighed. "Tom leaped to the conclusion, and I wasn't sure what to do about it. My acquaintance with Marcus is fast convincing me that my social skills are sadly lacking."

"But what am I supposed to talk to him about?" Peggy wailed.

"Just don't mention bodies in Mississippi," Ann grimaced.

"Bodies in . . . is he strange?"

"Hell, yes, he's strange!" Ann groaned. "But he's not nuts. He just drives other people that way."

"So why'd you invite him?" Peggy asked reasonably.

"I didn't invite him. He invited himself. He's very..." She trailed off uncertainly. "It's just that . . . he's the social equivalent of amoral."

"Huh?"

"You know. Immoral is when you know something is wrong and do it anyway. Amoral is when you do the same thing, but don't know that it's wrong."

"No, I didn't know that." Peggy grinned. "And I didn't care, either. You can call it what you want, but the results are the same."

"Maybe." Ann frowned. "But . . . I like him. He's . . ."

"Is he a good catch?" Peggy asked practically.

"I said I liked him. I didn't say I wanted to marry him."

"Yes, but—"

"But nothing. You try matchmaking, and I'll never bring anyone with me again," Ann warned. "Right now I don't have time to get involved with a man on anything but a very superficial level. Later, when my classes are finished and I've got a real job in computers and things aren't so hectic, then I'll look around for a meaningful relationship."

"I think—"

"Peggy, Ann—" Tom stuck his head in the kitchen "—get your purses and let's go." He withdrew as suddenly as he had come.

Good Lord, Ann thought in dismay. Marcus must have said something outrageous to have produced that kind of reaction.

"Go?" Peggy stopped washing the lettuce and stared blankly at Ann. "Go where? And what about lunch?" She gestured toward the steaming casserole.

"I don't know any more than you do, but I suppose we'd better find out." She went into the hallway to find the two men standing by the front door. Tom was jiggling his car keys impatiently.

"Where are we going?" Ann asked.

"To Yankee Stadium. Marcus has the use of a box behind the visitors' dugout this weekend," Tom said.

"He does?" Ann blinked in surprise.

"A friend of mine owns it, and he's in Europe this weekend," Marcus added.

"You like baseball?"

"Of course, doesn't everyone?" Marcus looked surprised at the question.

"No. I for one have never even seen a ball game," Ann replied, trying to integrate the unlikely fact that Marcus was a baseball fan with what else she knew about him.

"Then you're in for a real treat." Marcus smiled at her as if he really believed it.

"But what about lunch?" Peggy asked. "It's all ready."

"I'll buy you all the hot dogs you can eat," Tom offered. "Just hurry up. It'll take awhile to get to the Bronx at this time of day, and I don't want to miss the start of the game."

"But what about the boys?" Peggy cried. "Remember your sons?"

"Of course I remember them." Tom looked exasperated by such denseness. "Heather next door is going to keep an eye on them, and in exchange you're going to keep her five overnight next Saturday."

"Lovely," Peggy muttered as she picked up her purse and followed her husband out the door.

Ann trailed along behind still unable to picture Marcus at a ball game. One thing was certain, life around him was certainly never dull!

5

"HERE, TOM." Marcus handed him the pass once they were in Yankee Stadium. "You and Peggy use the box. Ann and I will meet you here after the game."

"But I can't take your tickets!" Tom protested. "I thought we'd all fit into the box."

"We would," Marcus agreed. "But this is Ann's first ball game."

"So?" Ann asked.

"So everyone's first game should be viewed from the bleachers. It's part of the mystique."

"Maybe for you..." Ann began, seeing her hope of at least getting to pass part of a boring afternoon talking to Peggy disappearing.

"He's got a point, Ann," Tom conceded. "The bleachers are where you first catch baseball fever."

"And heaven knows what else," Ann mumbled under her breath as she watched Peggy being dragged away by her husband.

"See you after the game," Peggy called back.

"Two bleacher seats, please." Marcus handed a bill to the ticket seller and received two tickets in exchange. "Come on, Ann." He hurried her along. "The game's due to start any minute."

"Mustn't miss the kickoff," she muttered, and began trotting along beside him. She came to a surprised stop as they emerged from the tunnel into the bright sunshine. Directly in front of her was what seemed to be acres and acres of immaculately manicured lawn. All that bright greenness hidden away in the midst of the city's black pavement and gray concrete was a pleasant shock.

"You have all the earmarks of a dedicated Yankee fan," Marcus approved of her reaction.

"Don't hold your breath," she said dryly. "The last sporting event I saw was a high school football game."

"Rather like me and the last time I read fiction."

"It's hardly the same thing." Ann followed him as he began to climb the steps leading to their seats.

"Why not? Both fiction and sports are integral parts of our culture. Both provide entertainment."

"But reading also provides facts." She sank down into the hard seat that Marcus pointed to.

"Not fiction," he objected. "Fiction tells you things like it's fine to drag a body around Mississippi in July."

"Will you shut up about that damned body!" Ann froze when the elderly woman in front of them recoiled in obvious horror at her words. The woman peered fearfully at Marcus, her eyes lingering on the impressive swell of his biceps under his short sleeves.

Ann took a deep breath, trying to decide how to remedy the situation. Clearly she had to say something. The poor woman looked terrified. "Umm, the body he mentioned . . ."

"It's none of my business, I'm sure." The woman picked up the bag at her feet and scuttled out into the aisle. "I was just moving."

"You see—" Marcus watched the woman rush away "—someone else who doesn't like Faulkner. But don't feel badly that not everyone shares your taste in literature," he comforted her. "That's what makes people interesting, being different."

"Take my word for it, Marcus," she stated decisively. "There's a limit as to how far that analogy extends."

"There are always limits. The trick is to try to expand them." His eyes gleamed, and he studied her lips with a disturbing intensity. "I wonder what yours are?" he murmured, his attention slipping lower, down past her neck, coming to rest on the soft swell of her breasts.

A flash of excitement swirled through her as she basked in the approving light glowing in his eyes. "I'd say you're definitely pushing the limits. At least for the bleachers."

"Mmm." He looked around at the kids populating the seats. "You could be right. We'll discuss it in greater detail later." His eyes flared and her stomach lurched, anticipation spiraling through her.

"Ha! There we go." Marcus suddenly stood, and Ann looked up at him in confusion. "The 'Star Spangled Banner.'" He hauled her to her feet.

Ann cocked her head to one side and listened. "Are you sure that's what the cacophony of sound is?"

"A little more respect, please. This is serious."

"Nine men trying to smash a little white ball!" She sank back down into the seat as the last notes of the song were swallowed up in the appreciative roar of the crowd.

"There's a lot more to baseball than trying to hit a ball," he reproved. "It's an art."

"I read an article in the paper yesterday that claimed pornography was an art form," she said tartly. "But that doesn't make it so."

"Pornography?" he repeated thoughtfully. "An art form?"

She groaned inwardly as she watched his eyes narrow in sudden interest. Too late, she remembered his disconcerting habit of suddenly focusing his whole attention on something she'd said. Why had she mentioned anything as inflammatory as pornography, she asked herself in resignation?

"I was being flip. Forget it. What's the pitcher doing?" She had tried to divert him, but Marcus seemed to follow only one line of thought at a time.

"That's an intriguing supposition."

"What? The pitcher?"

"An art form. Were they relating this information to our culture?"

"Yours or mine?" she snapped. "I'm beginning to think that you belong to a subculture. A very sub-subculture!"

"Of course I do. So do you. Our sex alone would guarantee that. Which brings us back to your pornography."

Ann gritted her teeth in exasperation. Gladys hadn't been exaggerating the least bit when she'd likened him to a bulldog. She'd never met anyone with his single-mindedness before.

"Listen to me very carefully, Marcus." She took a deep breath and slowly exhaled it. "I should never have brought the subject up in the first place, but I certainly didn't expect to discuss it in the bleachers."

"Where did you expect to discuss it?"

"Nowhere!" she enunciated. "It is not a subject one discusses."

Marcus's bright blue eyes narrowed, and he studied her flushed face with such speculative interest that she became very uneasy. Suddenly there was the loud crack as the ball hit the bat, followed by the roar of the crowd.

"Oh, what happened, Marcus?" she exclaimed, trying again to divert him, but he didn't even glance toward the field.

"You know, Ann," he said slowly, "I'm beginning to think that underneath your sensual exterior lurks an incipient prude."

Sensual exterior? The phrase clogged her thought processes so that it was a second before the last part of his sentence penetrated.

"I am not!"

"Sensual, or a prude?" He tipped his head to one side and studied the hectic flush staining her cheekbones with a detachment that infuriated her.

"I am a perfectly normal, conventional—" she favored him with a meaningful glare "—person. Unlike some people I see."

"Hmm." He casually looked around the bleachers. "Perhaps, but going to a ball game on a Saturday afternoon is pretty conventional behavior in and of itself."

"You're here!"

"See, that proves it." He beamed at her.

"Oh!" Ann sputtered.

"Are you a prude?" Tenaciously he returned to the subject.

"Prude is a highly subjective term with a great deal of individual connotations. Since I don't know exactly how you define the term, I can hardly say, can I?"

"A valid point," he conceded. "And quite surprising."

"My point?"

"No, that you made it. I couldn't help but notice that you aren't the most logical of women. We can explore my exact conception of prudery later tonight, and you can tell me what you think."

"What I think is as X-rated as the blasted pornography! No!" She realized her mistake when his eyes began to gleam again. "The subject is closed."

"Postponed for a more thorough discussion at a later date," he corrected.

"Whatever, all I know is that you dragged me to this game, and the least you can do is let me watch it."

Marcus glanced down at the green field as if surprised to discover himself in a ballpark. "The least?"

"And the most is to get me a hot dog and a cold drink."

"Certainly." He gestured toward the vendor at the end of the aisle. "What do you want on it?"

"Everything." She smiled, beginning to enjoy herself. The sun was deliciously hot, the air reasonably clean, she was with a man she really liked—although heaven only knew why—and she was about to get something to eat that wasn't peanut butter.

"Thanks." She accepted the paper-wrapped hot dog and the huge icy soda. "It looks delicious."

"It is," he agreed. "Nothing tastes quite like a hot dog eaten with a ball game in front of it."

Ann happily munched her way through the hot dog, a package of potato chips, a box of caramel corn and quaffed two drinks. Finally, absolutely replete, she stuffed the trash, to be disposed of on the way out, into her purse.

Her eyes brightened as she saw the copy of *The Phaedo* she'd bought that morning. She stole a glance at Marcus to find that his attention was firmly centered on the ball game. She followed his gaze down onto the field, watching the white-suited player on first dancing up and down as if the ground under his feet was on fire. As she continued to watch, the pitcher threw the ball to first and the man dived headfirst into the base.

She shook her head in disgust while he stood up and began to brush the dirt off the front of his shirt. What a mess! Whoever had said that men were simply little boys in bigger bodies must have been watching some kind of ball game at the time. Ah well, to each his own. She pulled out her book and opened it with a feeling of anticipation. An anticipation that was never realized. One large hand suddenly closed over the printed page and plucked the book out of her grasp.

"Hey!" Ann objected as Marcus closed it and put it back in her purse.

"You expect me to read that book you foisted off on me, don't you?"

"Yes, but what's that got to do with anything?"

"If I can suffer through fiction, then you can at least give the ball game a sporting chance."

"All right." Her innate sense of honesty made her admit the validity of his statement. "But you promise to read it?"

"Scout's honor."

"Were you a Scout?" she asked dubiously.

"Of course I was. I had a perfectly normal childhood."

"You mean, with parents and everything?" she teased.

"Not everything," he frowned. "I didn't have any siblings. I was all alone except for Judas."

"Judas?" Ann blinked. "Who on earth would name a kid Judas."

"Not a kid, a dog, and I named him. I felt sorry for him."

"The dog?"

"No, Judas Iscariot."

"You did? Why on earth would you feel sorry for him?"

"Because if Jesus were to rise again, then he had to be killed, right?"

"Yes," she agreed, not seeing what he was getting at.

"And in order to be killed, someone had to betray him. So the whole thing hinges on someone betraying him."

"I guess."

"Therefore, in essence, it was preordained that Judas would be a traitor. He was, in effect, set up."

"But . . ." She paused uncertainly. "But he didn't have to do it."

"Someone did," Marcus insisted. "Someone had to be the one to point the finger. Someone had to be the villain in order to make it all work right."

"That's an interesting philosophical question," she conceded, "but I don't know enough about religion to argue it."

"From what I've seen, lack of knowledge hasn't stopped people from arguing religion before."

"I am not 'people.' I am me."

"True." His eyes were frankly approving. "And a very nice me you are, too."

His admiring words accelerated her heartbeat, and she rushed into speech. "So you were an only child?"

"Umm. I always wanted lots of brothers and sisters."

"Do you have any children?" she heard herself ask with dismay. She knew she had no right to ask him personal questions. No right, but an overwhelming desire to know, regardless.

"No." He didn't seem to find anything strange about her curiosity. "But I fully intend to have a family."

And presumably a wife, she told herself, the thought inexplicably deflating her. What did she care if he got married? The poor woman deserved her sympathy, not the momentary flash of envy she'd felt. When she landed a job in computers, had a new apartment and her life was arranged exactly as she wanted it, then she'd look around for a perfect mate. Something Marcus would never be. Not that she cared. As a friend, as someone to discuss things with, he was fine.

To her relief, the man in the white pin-striped suit at home plate belted the ball into the bleachers at that precise moment. In the ensuing excitement, the disquieting subject was dropped.

Two hours later, Ann was more than ready to leave. Her nose and cheekbones were burned a bright cherry red and all the cheering had given her a headache. But all things considered, she'd rather enjoyed herself. Certainly more than she'd ever expected to.

Marcus guided her toward the exit. "How'd you like it?"

"Not bad." She sidestepped a young boy running past her. "The hot dogs were great, the sunshine was marvelous and the game itself was a lot like reading Dickens."

"What?"

"Sure, Dickens got paid by the word, and since he was spending a fortune doing up his estate, he naturally used lots of words."

"I knew there was a reason I didn't like Dickens," Marcus said.

"You can hardly single him out for that distinction," Ann said dryly. "You don't like any real authors. Yet," she added with a crusading gleam in her eye. "Anyway, in my opinion both Dickens and baseball would be better condensed to about half. It's incredible the amount of time they take to play this game."

"That's part of the strategy," he objected.

"What strategy?" she scoffed. "That the batter will get so bored waiting for the pitch that he'll fall asleep?"

"It throws them off balance."

"I will admit that the game is off balance. Did you realize that the pitcher threw to first base twenty-eight times when that guy was on in the seventh inning?"

"That guy happens to be one of the fastest base runners in the league."

"Big deal." She wasn't impressed. "I could have made it to second after the pitcher finally threw the ball into right field."

"That was unfortunate," he admitted.

"The manager certainly seemed to think so." Ann chuckled at the memory of the way the man had come bounding out of the dugout to remove the pitcher. "But my point is that he wasted twenty-eight pitches. If he hadn't thrown them, the game would have ended fifteen minutes earlier."

"If he hadn't thrown them, the man would have stolen second base," Marcus objected.

"Which would have been an improvement since he wound up on third because of the wild pitch!"

"You don't understand the strategy," he repeated.

"Maybe not, but I understand the results. Oh, look. There's Tom and Peggy." Ann waved wildly to get their attention.

"Maybe we should try a night game," Marcus mused, and Ann felt her spirits lift at his intention of inviting her out again.

"They were great seats!" Tom began enthusing the minute he reached them. "Absolutely great. We were almost mowed down by foul balls twice!"

"Good Lord." Ann was shocked.

Peggy laughed at Ann's worried expression. "He considers that a plus."

"Sure is." Tom grinned broadly. "I've never been that close to the action before."

"I'll call you the next time I get the use of the box," Marcus offered.

Although she didn't for a moment doubt that he meant it, Ann was surprised at his offer. Marcus had probably never even heard of a social lie, let alone used one.

"Great!" Tom enthused. "How about if we go back home and sample Peggy's casserole?"

"Yes, please come," Peggy seconded the invitation.

"First let me call the lab," Marcus said. "There ought to be some results from what I started this morning." He stopped in front of the row of public phones.

Ann leaned back against the wall and frankly eavesdropped on his conversation. Not that she got much information from Marcus's muttered monosyllables. She watched as he replaced the phone and stared at it. His eyes were narrowed, and he appeared to be deep in thought. Whatever the lab had told him had destroyed his happy mood.

"Well?" Tom demanded. "Did you get that cleared up?"

Marcus blinked and glanced vaguely at him. "Unfortunately not. The blood counts are all wrong, considering."

Considering what? Ann wondered, but didn't ask. Even if he came out of his preoccupation long enough to tell her, she'd never understand his explanation.

"I'll have to go back. It was nice meeting you." He gave the Walkers an absent smile, took Ann's arm and started toward the exit.

"But you came in our car," Tom called after him, but Marcus didn't hear him.

"Why would they be double what they should be?" he queried as he hailed a taxi and hustled Ann into it.

"Where to, buddie?" The cabbie started the meter.

Ann listened in surprise as he gave her address. Marcus might have relegated her to the back of his mind, but he hadn't forgotten her altogether. The small victory warmed her, and she sank back against the seat, reconciled to the abrupt ending of her day.

"GLADYS," ANN SAID, frowning worriedly into her friend's pale, drawn face, "why don't you go on home. All that's left are the few offices at the end of the hall."

Gladys hesitated. "I shouldn't . . ."

"What you shouldn't have done was come in in the first place."

"It's just that my sinuses are bothering me. It happens every once in a while, and there's nothing to do but to suffer through the headache."

"I hesitate to suggest such a novel approach, but have you ever considered seeing a doctor?"

"After watching the ones here! Not unless I was dying!" She shook her head emphatically, then moaned when the action exasperated the pain.

"Go on. Go home and go to bed," Ann urged. "It won't take me half an hour to finish."

"Thanks." Gladys gave her a weak smile. "I think I will."

Ann watched as Gladys disappeared around the corner, and then she pushed the cleaning cart to the end of the hallway. A sense of excitement spiraled through her as she read the nameplate on Marcus's door, wondering if he was behind it. His lights were still on, but that didn't mean a whole lot. The vast majority of researchers at the institute never turned anything off.

Nervously she studied the thin bar of light under the door. She hadn't seen him since he'd deposited her on her doorstep after the ball game on Saturday. She hadn't had so much as a glimpse of him in four days. Deciding to postpone the moment, she hurriedly swept and dusted the other two offices before returning to Marcus's.

Ann ran suddenly damp palms over her denim-clad thighs and, taking a deep breath, rapped decisively on the pale oak door. There was no answer. She refused to even acknowledge the disappointment that flooded her; she told herself that she was pleased, that a vacant office would be quicker to clean and she would get home earlier. Home to her empty apartment, the unbidden thought surfaced, but she quickly denied it. It wasn't empty—Serendipity was there. A smile teased her lips at the thought of the ridiculous little rodent. She turned the knob and flung open the door, coming to a surprised halt.

Marcus was there! He was seated behind his desk reading a book, his large Adidas-clad feet propped up in the middle of an incredible stack of litter.

Ann cleared her throat and, when he took no notice of her, pushed the cart into the room and closed the door behind her. Uncertainly she studied him, her eyes lingering on the disheveled black hair that looked as if he'd been running impatient fingers through it. An adventurous strand had tumbled down over his broad forehead, and as she watched he flicked it aside.

She opened her mouth, but hesitated. Should she call him Marcus, or should she use the more formal Dr. Blackmore since they were in the institute? Always provided she could even get his attention, a rueful smile curved her lips. Maybe she should simply hit him over the head. Or else touch something on his desk; she remembered how he'd reacted the last time she'd done that.

"Marcus..." she tried, and got absolutely no response. Piqued, she decided to ignore his presence and clean around him, waiting for the noise to disturb his concentration.

To her amazement, he didn't even seem to notice when she ran the sweeper or flicked the feather duster over the filing cabinets. She eyed him in disbelief. Surely he couldn't block out everything happening around him. Concentration was fine, but Marcus was well on his way to turning a virtue into a vice. What would happen if they had a fire? She watched in exasperation as he turned another page. He'd never even hear the alarm. He'd simply sit there while the flames... She hurriedly shut out the awful thought. It couldn't happen anyway, she assured herself. The institute had a great sprinkling system. She glanced up at the ceiling. He'd simply get very wet.

She pressed her lips together; if Marcus wanted to imitate the furniture, then she'd treat him that way. She picked up the feather duster and began to dust his feet. She worked her way up over his calves, flicked quickly over his muscular thighs, her eyes lingering momentarily on the masculine swell beneath his jeans before moving upward over his flat stomach.

"What are you doing?" he asked calmly as she dusted his left bicep with meticulous care.

"It speaks!" She fell back in simulated horror.

"It does a whole lot more than speak." His large hand suddenly reached out and grabbed her arm, tumbling her into his lap. She landed across his hard thighs and found herself staring into his bright blue eyes.

Marcus plucked the feather duster out of her hand and tossed it onto the floor. "Good evening, Ann."

"Are you sure?" She grinned at him. "As deeply as you were absorbed in that book, it could be tomorrow morning."

"It can't be past eleven because that's when you get off work and, besides, it's all your fault."

"Ah, yes." She nodded sagely. "The eternal masculine cry. But I fail to see how this could even possibly be construed as my fault."

"It was that book you forced on me." He leaned forward and picked it up off the desk.

Ann gulped; his movement had pressed his upper body firmly onto her. She breathed deeply, savoring the heady aroma emanating from him. He was wearing a different after-shave, she realized, and sniffed again. It smelled delicious. She allowed her body to relax into him.

Marcus leaned back and, comfortably settling her body against his broad chest, showed her the book he'd been reading.

Ann shook herself free from the hypnotic beat of his heart, which was reverberating through her body, and took a closer look at the paperback. "Oh, the science-fiction book. No wonder you were enthralled."

"Try appalled," he corrected. "This is the most idiotic drivel that I've ever read."

"What could possibly be wrong with it?"

"What isn't wrong!" He opened the book to the table of contents, and Ann shivered as the muscles in his encircling arms rippled. "Take this first gem," he offered in disgust. "Aliens suddenly make a man grow to a hundred feet, and the guy runs around being superman!"

"You object to good deeds?"

"I object to stupidity! Do you have any idea what would happen to his bone structure if a man suddenly became a hundred feet tall? His ankles would snap, and that would just be the start of his problems."

"So one story didn't work out."

"And then, in this next one, the author has skin divers working at the bottom of the Marianas Trench wearing nothing but rubber suits."

"So?" she responded blankly.

"The pressure would turn them into mush."

"Oh."

"And in the next story, the spaceship's traveling faster than the speed of light. That's impossible because as a body approaches the speed of light its mass increases disproportionately, and it would turn itself into energy."

"Of course," she marveled. "Why didn't I think of that?"

"And this next one has a gigantic ship entering the earth's atmosphere at tremendous speeds. It would burn up because any metal strong enough to take the pressure would be too heavy to get off the ground in the first place."

Ann tipped her head back and stared up into his annoyed face. "Marcus, you know too much for your own good. You're supposed to suspend disbelief while you read these."

"I don't mind suspending it, but you have to draw the line somewhere."

"Surely one of them was based on a feasible concept?"

"Hmmm." His eyes began to gleam with a light she instinctively mistrusted. "Well, now that you mention it, one of them did present a concept that might be worth exploring."

"Oh?" Her gaze was riveted to the firm line of his square chin. A dark shadow colored his jaw, and she felt her fingers tingle at the thought of touching the abrasive surface.

"Yes, but I'll need some cooperation," he murmured as his fingers captured her soft chin and he tilted her head back over his upper arm.

"Umm, well . . ." Her stomach twisted as his thumb began to gently rub back and forth over her lower lip. "I...ah..." She trembled as he cradled her body against his chest, his hand coming to rest beneath the soft swell of her breast. Her breathing developed an uneven cadence, and she was having trouble forming a coherent thought.

Mesmerized, she watched his head descend, and then his mouth met hers. A feeling of inevitability swept through her at the contact, and she closed her eyes to better focus on her heightened sensibilities. Her fingers tentatively crept up to caress his neck, then gaining confidence, twined themselves in the silken strands of his thick black hair.

His emerging beard brushed over her tender cheek, and tiny rivulets of awareness radiated from the point of contact. She reacted instinctively, opening her mouth to welcome him, then delicately fencing with his tongue, moaning exultantly at the delectable sensations their dueling engendered. Marcus greedily drank the inarticulate sounds of pleasure from her lips.

Ann gasped as his hand suddenly slipped beneath her T-shirt. His fingers splayed possessively over her rib cage and she shifted restively, the hard burning warmth of him beneath her soft hips telling her that he was as affected by the kiss as she was. A fact that made her fiercely glad. She wanted him to be as enmeshed in what was happening as she was.

He swiftly dealt with the clasp on her bra, and she felt it slip loose a second before his hand captured her soft flesh. "Marcus!" His name escaped on a strangled gasp, and she burrowed her head into his shoulder.

"You're so soft." His voice soothed even as his touch was driving her into a frenzy of longing. He caught her nipple between his thumb and forefinger and gently tugged.

A convulsive shudder shook her, momentarily freeing her from the sensual web he was weaving. A feeling akin to panic washed over her at her headlong response to him. It wasn't like her, she thought frantically. None of this was. It was all too much. Too much and too fast, and she had to stop it now while she still could.

"No," she blurted out. "I don't want . . ."

"It's all right." Marcus's husky voice reassured her. "I'm not trying to push you into anything you don't want. We have all the time in the world."

We do? She wondered distractedly as his capable hands refastened her bra, pulled her T-shirt down and then tugged her head into his shoulder. His hand stroked slowly over her back, but there was a different quality to his caress this time. Now, his fingers were soothing not arousing, and Ann felt her tense muscles begin to relax.

"What scientific principle?" She finally remembered what they'd been talking about.

"Time travel."

"Time travel?" she repeated. "How does..." She paused, uncertain of exactly what to call what they'd been sharing.

"Kissing," Marcus supplied. "We were kissing. You know, Ann, for an adult woman who claims she isn't a prude, your education has been sadly lacking."

Calling what she and Marcus had shared kissing was like calling a tornado a windstorm, she thought. And they had been sharing; the indisputable fact warmed her. Marcus had also derived pleasure from their embrace.

She felt obligated to point out that she was not a prude. "And you still haven't answered my question. What's kissing got to do with time travel?" she added.

"In order for time travel to work, two objects must occupy the same space at the same time."

"Same space?" she asked, then felt a warmth stain her cheeks as the full impact of what he was saying struck. "Marcus, you're impossible! Didn't you enjoy any of the stories?"

"No, they aren't the least bit scientific," he defended himself. "Of course, I still have one more to go." He looked crestfallen at the admission.

"Forget it," she grimaced. "It's obvious that science fiction isn't your thing."

"I could have told you that. As a matter of fact, I did."

"But something has to be," she argued, ignoring his regrettable tendency to say I told you so. "It's simply a question of finding it."

"I don't suppose you'd be willing to wait until it found us?"

"Not a chance."

"I didn't really think so," he admitted with a sigh. "You know, stubbornness is not an attractive trait in a woman."

"In anyone." She favored him with a knowing stare.

He grinned at her. "Am I to take that personally?"

"I live in hope." She regretfully moved off his lap. "I'd better get this stuff put away."

"I'll drop you off on my way home."

His offhand suggestion warmed her.

6

"THERE YOU ARE," Marcus observed from the door of one of the lab rooms on the second floor.

Ann looked at him over the top of the broom she was pushing, pausing a moment to savor the surge of pleasure that engulfed her at the sight of his broad frame. Her eyes lingered on his thick black hair, which was endearingly rumpled, before falling lower to become entrapped in the glimmering depths of his eyes. She told herself to calm down as her heart responded to the twinkling lights she discovered there. After all, she had seen the man just last night . . . and kissed him. The memory made her heart beat even faster.

She forced a prosaic response. "Where else should I be?"

"At ten-forty you're usually doing the offices at my end of the hall. You've changed your schedule," he accused.

"Not really, it was just that Dr. Andrews in the office beside you asked us to do that end during dinner because he's working late and didn't want to be disturbed." She found herself explaining when what she really wanted to do was ask him why he'd learned her schedule.

"Disturbed?"

"Umm. Not everyone is blessed with your powers of concentration."

"Do I hear an echo of a pious 'thank goodness' in the air?" He grinned at her.

"If the shoe fits . . ." She grinned back.

"Nonsense. You can do better than that."

"Better than what?"

"Than a cliché. Clichés are the result of a stagnating intellect."

"Or association with one," she retaliated.

"Hmm." He used the manila folder he was carrying to scratch his chin, and Ann shivered at the faint raspy sound his emerging beard made as it scraped over the cardboard. "An interesting concept. We'll discuss it over a meal when you've finished."

"Are you inviting me or telling me?" Her calm voice effectively masked the excitement bubbling through her.

"Inviting. Never would I presume to dictate to such a lovely lady."

"Talk about clichés." She rolled her eyes.

"You're right." He looked thoughtful. "They must be contagious. I'll meet you in the front lobby at eleven."

"I'll be there," she called after his retreating back. Blasted man. He could have at least waited for her answer instead of automatically assuming that she'd accept. But then, after the way she'd responded to him last night, he could be forgiven for presuming that she wasn't averse to his company.

"I sure hope you know what you're doing." Gladys's disapproving voice startled Ann, and she hurriedly turned to her friend. In her excitement at seeing Marcus, she'd forgotten that Gladys was cleaning behind the cabinets.

"What? Going out for a snack? It's no big deal."

"I know it, and I'll lay odds that Dr. Blackmore knows it," Gladys said. "The question is do you?"

"Rest assured, my friend." Ann began to push her broom again. "I'm too old to start weaving romantic daydreams around Marcus Blackmore. He's simply a friend."

"No woman is ever too old," Gladys said firmly. "Just because your ex-husband gave you a bad time is no reason for you to be sour on all men."

"Steve didn't give me a bad time. At least not from his point of view," Ann responded fairly. "And simply because I don't see a man as the answer to all life's problems doesn't mean that I'm soured on them."

"So you say, but I still don't believe that modern drivel that men and women can be friends."

"Gladys, don't tell me that you're secretly harboring a grand passion for Dr. Blackmore?" Ann deliberately turned the conversation along lighter lines. She didn't want to discuss her relationship with Marcus. Not that she was sure what they shared could be called a relationship.

"Why shouldn't I? At least it'd be more normal than your claiming he's just a friend. Although it's strange," Gladys mused, "the way you talk to him."

"The way I talk to him? What do you mean?"

"I'm not sure exactly. Kind of like you think you're as good as he is."

"Wrong. I think I'm better," Ann countered dryly.

"No, I mean smart-wise. He's so clever."

"Only about biochemistry. About fiction he's appallingly ignorant," Ann informed her. "But since the sum total of my knowledge of chemistry is that H^2O stands for water, I simply avoid the subject."

"Maybe...." Gladys turned back to her dusting. "But I still think you'd have been better off with my cousin's boy."

An hour later, Ann was willing to concede that Gladys may have been right. She shifted restlessly on the brown leather chair facing the elevator, willing Marcus to appear.

"Waiting for a ride, Miss Somerton?" asked the elderly guard who sat at the reception desk.

"Yes, I'm waiting." She forced a smile, then glanced back at the large wall clock. Eleven-forty and Marcus still wasn't here!

Perhaps he'd run into trouble with an experiment. She tried to reassure herself, but her knowledge of medical research was so sketchy that she didn't even know if that was a feasible excuse. *Quit trying to kid yourself*, she thought disconsolately. *He's plain forgotten that he invited you out.* Even if he was busy he could have called down to the reception desk and asked the guard to tell her that he'd been delayed.

A feeling of déjà vu swept over her as she watched the hypnotic sweep of the second hand. Countless times it seemed she had sat in her kitchen watching the clock and wondering if Steve was ever going to come home. She tried to convince herself it wasn't the same. Her ex-husband had invariably been out with the boys at a local bar, while Marcus was undoubtedly working on something that would eventually be of enormous benefit to mankind.

The knowledge gave her no comfort, since whatever the motivation the results were the same. She had been forgotten. She had put up with it from Steve because she had had no choice, but that was hardly the case with Marcus. She had more pride than to simply sit here and wait in the vague hope that he might eventually remember she existed. She pursed her lips in anger. Enough was enough. She'd already waited forty-five minutes. It was late, and she had classes in the morning. She wasn't going to sit here another second.

Resolutely, she got to her feet and marched across the lobby, ignoring her craven impulse to go up to his office and see if he was there. Even the knowledge that she was doing the right thing didn't make up for the feeling of disappointment that engulfed her the moment she walked through the front door.

By morning Ann had managed to convince herself that Marcus's forgetting her was for the best. That her pleasure at finding someone to talk to had temporarily eclipsed the danger Marcus represented to both her hard-won peace of mind and her hectic schedule. She knew she would be much wiser to distance herself from him now before he did it for her later.

Which made it all the more frustrating when her heart began to race and her mouth went dry when she stepped off the elevator and caught sight of him sitting in the deserted front lobby as she left work Friday night. Until she'd met Marcus, she'd never been in a situation where her emotions had acted independently of her mind, and she found it very disconcerting. She tried to still her wayward body's response to him.

She paused, uncertain of what do do, and the elevator doors slid shut behind her. She could pretend that last night had never happened and greet him accordingly, or she could give in to the ignoble impulse to tell him exactly what she thought of him for leaving her cooling her heels in the lobby for the better part of an hour.

She regretfully decided that yelling at him might relieve her feelings of frustration, but it might also give him the idea that she was reading more into their casual dates than he'd intended. The last thing she wanted was for him to think that she was one of those pathetic women who viewed all men as potential husbands.

But, then, maybe he wasn't waiting for her at all. The possibility chilled her. There could be lots of perfectly incomprehensible reasons why Marcus was sitting in a deserted lobby at eleven o'clock at night. Taking a deep breath, she started across the lobby, intending to bestow a gracious nod on Marcus as she passed him.

Marcus, however, had other ideas. He rose when she reached his chair and gave her a warm smile.

"Good evening, Ann."

"Hi." She was unable to keep a certain coolness out of her voice despite the fact that he'd finally managed to come up with a conventional greeting. How dared he ignore her one night and expect a warm welcome the next?

"Bad day?" he sympathized.

"Today wasn't as bad as last night," she stated significantly, but her meaning escaped him entirely.

"Mmmm, we all have days like that."

And if I continue to see you, I'm going to have lots of them, she thought ruefully. She searched the warmly sympathetic depths of his blue eyes. The wretched man didn't even remember that he'd stood her up! An unexpected rush of frustration made her clench her teeth. She wasn't even going to get an apology!

"You *have* had a bad day. You're very tense. Come on. I'll buy you a pizza. I know a great little place over on Twenty-third Street that serves the best pepperoni pizza with double cheese you ever tasted."

The impulse to frustrate him was irresistible. "I don't want pepperoni."

"You can choose," he offered with a promptness that made her feel ashamed of herself. She was being obstructive to punish him for something that he didn't even remember doing. It was not only petty, but totally fruitless.

"How about if we get half pepperoni and half mushroom and sausage?" she offered, slipping through the door he held open.

"With double cheese," he agreed, waving at a taxi, which cruised to a halt in front of them.

"That's amazing," she marveled, climbing into the back seat.

"What?" Marcus looked confused.

"The way that taxi appeared the minute we wanted it. I thought that only happened in the movies."

He gave the address to the cabbie and turned back to her. "It happens all the time if you call ahead."

"And here I thought you had the magic touch." Ann laughed, pleasure replacing her lingering pique. He'd not only planned to take her out, he'd even remembered to call a taxi. He wasn't totally hopeless. Just partially.

"Oh, I most definitely have a magic touch." He gave her a slow smile that shortened her breath. Basking in the warmth of the approval shining in his glowing eyes, she felt like an entirely different person from the calm, rational individual she knew herself to be. She felt feminine and desired. She was so busy savoring the heady sensation that she barely noticed when Marcus paid the cabbie and helped her out.

"As much as you use cabs, Marcus, you really ought to get a car. It'd be much cheaper in the long run."

"Not if you take my peace of mind into consideration," he replied. "I don't know what it is about machines, but they take one look at me and then roll over and die. Usually at the most inconvenient moment possible."

"Now there's a scientific explanation if ever I heard one," she scoffed.

"It's true," he insisted. "Some things defy logic."

"And you head the list." She surveyed the line of people waiting to be seated. "You know, Marcus, I'm not sure I'm hungry enough to wait that long."

"And I'm too hungry to wait that long. Let's get a take-out order and eat at my place." He moved toward the cash register.

Said the spider to the fly, she thought fatalistically and trailed along behind him. She knew she shouldn't go. Not after her explosive reaction to his kiss on Wednesday. It was asking for trouble. They'd be alone. Just the two of them. And in circumstances that would make it easy for a kiss to develop into a whole lot more.

Ann moistened her lips with the tip of her tongue, images of just what a whole lot more could entail flooding her mind. Speculatively, she studied his broad shoulders and measured the inherent strength in his muscular arms. Her glance dropped to his long brown fingers lying on the black Formica counter. She remembered the feel of those fingers on her bare skin and a tremor chased over her. Rising excitement filled her. To heck with prudence and caution. She was an unattached adult woman, and if she chose to go home with Marcus she wasn't hurting anyone. Except, perhaps, herself. The unwelcome thought surfaced, but she refused to explore it.

By the time they reached his town house, Ann was a bundle of nerves. While she didn't regret her decision to return with him, she did regret her lack of experience in handling a situation like this. Always provided that there was a situation to handle. It was entirely possible that when he'd invited her home for a pizza, that's exactly what he'd meant.

She took a deep breath and started up the stairs to the top floor. She'd wait for him to make the first move, she decided. She was so deep in thought that she barely noticed when she tripped the electronic eye and the lights turned on.

She glanced around the large dusty room, looking for a table. There wasn't one. She eyed his desk speculatively, noting that the petrified banana peel was still there.

"Where do you eat?" she asked, knowing that the bedroom held a minimum of furniture.

"Out." He dropped the pizza carton on the chair and began to rummage through what appeared to be a box of trash. When he'd managed to scatter its entire contents on the floor, he looked around the room in annoyance. "I know it's here somewhere."

Ann picked up the pizza, frowning at the grease stains on the bottom of the box. She glanced down at the chair's cream-colored upholstery, relieved to see that it was unstained. Honestly, the man needed to be housebroken.

"Don't you ever eat in?" she persisted.

"Sometimes I bring home sandwiches," he murmured absently, then knocked over a four-foot-high stack of books while looking behind them.

"So where do you eat your sandwiches?"

"At my desk." He pulled back the curtains framing the huge front windows and looked behind them. He turned to find her studying the desk. "No, absolutely not! We can eat on the floor as soon as I find the wine."

"You're looking for wine behind the curtains!" she asked incredulously.

"Well, it's not out where you can see it," he defended himself.

Only the dust and litter was in plain sight, Ann thought acidly, but held her tongue. Being invited for a midnight snack didn't give her the right to criticize his housekeeping or lack thereof.

"I can't find it. It'll have to be Coke," he said in disgust.

"You haven't checked under the bed." She was unable to resist the gibe.

"The bed! Why would anyone keep wine under the bed?"

"Why would you keep it behind the curtains?" she countered.

"That's not the same thing at all. Wait a minute while I run down and get the drinks."

"Bring back a couple of plates and silverware, please," she called after him, to no avail. When he came pounding back up the stairs, he was carrying two cans of Coke and nothing else.

"No, plates?" she asked in resignation.

"Lucy left me lots of plates, but I haven't any dish soap and after a couple of years of sitting in the cabinets, they're kind of dirty."

She instantly dismissed his dirty plates as totally uninteresting. Who was Lucy and what was she doing leaving him plates? Ann studied the top of his dark head as he pulled the tabs off the cans and pondered how she could find out. She briefly considered asking him outright before dismissing the idea. There was no way to casually question him about his past love life.

"Thanks." She accepted the can he handed her and helped herself to a piece of the pizza, trying not to think about what the greasy bottom of the carton was doing to the pale carpet.

She sighed contentedly after swallowing the spicy food. "Delicious."

"Stick with me, babe, and I'll show you all the best places." He gave a terrible imitation of George Raft, and Ann burst into laughter.

"Stick to your research, Marcus, because you're never going to make it in show business."

"Do you think I'll make it anywhere?" The question was innocuous enough, but the tiny lights dancing deep in his eyes pointed to hidden meanings.

Ann felt pressure building in her chest and she glanced down at her pizza, blindly watching the cheese slip off one side. She wished she could make some teasing comment back, instead of sitting there like an unsophisticated lump.

"Your cheese is escaping." His prosaic words recalled her, and she hurriedly caught the errant strand on her tongue. To her relief, he changed the subject.

"Is tomorrow the Saturday after?"

"After what?" She blinked, momentarily lost.

"After payday. So that you go to the bookstore." He polished off his piece of pizza and eyed her sausage and mushroom half. "Share?" he asked hopefully.

"Help yourself." She waved at it. "There's enough here for half a dozen people."

"Only if they're skinny little things like you."

"If I hang around you for very long, I'll soon weigh two hundred pounds. And, no, payday isn't until the end of next week. You should know, everyone gets paid at the same time."

"Oh, my checks don't come here anymore. They go to my accountant. It got to be annoying without any lights."

"Without..." Ann frowned. "I'm sure that if I think about it long enough I'll get the connection, but why don't you save me the trouble and explain it."

"The electric company kept turning out the lights, and it was dark."

"A predictable sequence," she concurred. "But why would they turn out your lights?"

"The bills, of course."

"The..." She stared at his dark head. "Let me guess. They'd send you a bill and you'd put it on your desk, and it would never again see the light of day?"

"Or any other kind of light," he added morosely. "The electric company is very unreasonable."

"I can imagine."

"And rude." He frowned in remembered annoyance. "A friend of mine offered to hook into their computer banks and mark my bills paid, but I didn't take him up on it. I didn't want to have anything to do with computers, satisfying as it might have been to get the better of one."

"Boy, you have got it bad. I thought you'd have declined because it's highly illegal!"

"Anyway, Lucy gave me the name of an accountant. So now my checks go directly to him and he pays all the bills."

Lucy again. Ann frowned inwardly. "That was nice of her," she probed cautiously.

"Mmm." Marcus surreptitiously picked up another piece of the mushroom-and-sausage pizza. "She's a good egg."

Ann weighed his words, drawing comfort from them. A good egg didn't really sound like a romantic object, despite the fact that her name kept cropping up. She wondered if Lucy could be a relative, but resisted asking. She thoughtfully munched her way through a second piece of pizza and, replete, licked her fingers.

"More?" Marcus offered.

"No." She yawned. "It's well past midnight, and it's not really a good idea to eat too much right before bedtime."

"I never have any trouble." He bit into another piece.

"I don't think you've got a stomach," she said dryly. "You've been living on fast food too long. I shudder to think of what your cholesterol level is."

"In the lower one-half of one percent of the white, male population of my age group," he said smugly.

"It figures. You'll probably be like the four-pack-a-day cigarette smoker who lives to be ninety. I think I'll wash my hands."

"Sure, we can save this for breakfast." He dumped the carton on top of his desk.

Ann hurried into the bath and quickly rinsed her hands and washed the tomato smear off her chin. If she'd misunderstood his interest, then she wanted to get home and into bed as soon as possible. And, if she hadn't misunderstood

it, then she still wanted to get into bed as soon as possible.
And there was nothing wrong with that, she told herself
staunchly. She was an adult. She knew what she was doing.
She hoped.

Her stomach rolled. Pizza late at night on a nervous
stomach was not proving a happy combination. She swallowed, firmed her resolve and marched into the bedroom
to find Marcus stretched out on the oversize bed, his hands
behind his head.

She paused beside the bed and glanced down at him, her
eyes drawn to his broad chest by the way the thin material
of his shirt stretched over it. Frantically she searched for a
greeting equal to the occasion, but her mind remained discouragingly blank.

"Come here, my lovely." He reached a hand out for her,
and she stared at it in fascination.

"Ann?" He sat up and reached for her, tugging her down
onto the mattress beside him. He pulled her tense body
against him and tucked her head into his shoulder. "You
aren't afraid of me, are you?" His long fingers began to
stroke gently over her rigid back.

"Of course not. I would never have come back here with
you if I'd been afraid." She trembled slightly as his caressing hand started to massage the back of her neck.

"Then why are you so nervous?" He turned on his side
and pulled her against his chest.

Marcus cupped her cheek in his hard palm and used his
thumb to lever her chin upward. "I told you I wasn't into
ravishments." A gentle smile tilted his firm lips and she eyed
them longingly, remembering the feel of them pressed
against hers.

"The problem's not you," she blurted out. "It's just that
I don't know...I mean, I'm not sure—" She ground to a halt
and risked a look up into his eyes. This close she could see

tiny prisms of blue crystals surrounding the dark pupils. She watched in fascination as they reflected the dim light from the bedside lamp. She took a deep breath, holding it as the action forced her breasts into the hard wall of his chest. She could feel them expanding with pleasure and she momentarily became lost in the exquisite sensation.

"Exhale." The command reached her through the tingling in her ears.

"I know that," she muttered on a rush of air. "I was just . . ."

"Savoring the incomparable feeling of our bodies touching?" His hand slipped under her shirt, deftly unfastened her bra and then purposefully removed both garments.

Ann held her breath, resisting the impulse to cross her hands over her chest.

Slowly he fondled her breasts. His thumbs grazed over the dusky-pink centers, and he watched with total absorption as they puckered beneath his ministrations.

Her heart began to pound as he lowered his head and gently nuzzled the soft mounds. "Do you like this?" he murmured.

"Oh, yes!" she gasped, arching her chest into his softly nibbling lips, silently demanding more than his teasing action.

"What is it you want, my lovely," rasped his husky voice, his warm breath caressing her skin, intensifying the sensation his wandering lips were creating. "This, perhaps?" The tip of his tongue began to paint circles around the tight buds.

A tremor shook her at the erotic motion and she gripped his shoulders, trying to pull him closer. It was like trying to move a wall. Marcus wasn't to be rushed. Instead he methodically learned her soft curves with his tongue. Finally his warm mouth closed over one peak.

"Marcus!" His name escaped on a strangled cry. His fiery caresses had put a match to her inhibitions, and she gave free rein to the sizzling emotions surging through her. Frantically, she kneaded his shirt-covered back, wanting to feel his bare skin beneath her fingertips, but too disoriented to figure out how to accomplish it. Ann moaned in protest when he suddenly stilled and moved backwards. She felt bereft at the loss of his heavy warmth and instinctively reached for him.

Marcus caught her hand and, placing a warm kiss on her palm, laid it beside her body.

"I have to answer it. No one calls at this time of night for pleasure." He moved off the bed and hurried into the front room.

"Answer? Answer what?" Ann propped herself up on one elbow. Without the distraction of Marcus's presence, it immediately became apparent the phone was ringing. She heard it break off in midshriek, presumably when he answered it.

Ann swung her legs over the side of the bed and sat up. She felt confused and disoriented, and underlying that was raging thwarted desire. Her insides were twisted with longing, and she craved physical contact with Marcus with an intensity that frightened her. She wasn't a physical person. She knew that. But, somehow, in his arms a facet of her personality had emerged that she'd never before suspected, and she needed time to come to grips with her unexpected self-discovery.

Her bewildered gaze lit on the splash of color her red T-shirt made on the pale carpeting. She glanced down at herself, at her bare breasts. Hastily she refastened her bra and yanked her T-shirt on. She was brushing her fingers through her tangled hair when Marcus returned.

She watched him cross the room and knew immediately that the phone call had upset him. His eyes reflected the depth of his thoughts, and his face was creased, as if he was under incredible tension.

"I'm sorry, Ann, I have to go out."

"Certainly." She wondered what else to say. She didn't have the courage to try to penetrate his remote mood, nor the right. Her policy of no entanglements worked both ways. "I'll go out with you, and you can lock up behind us."

"No." His distracted blue gaze suddenly focused on her. "I don't have time to take you home, and I certainly don't want to spend the night wondering if you were mugged on your way."

"But . . ."

"You stay here, and I'll drop you off at your apartment tomorrow on my way to the airport."

"Airport?" she echoed.

"I have to go to Boston for two weeks," he replied shortly. "Promise you'll stay."

"All right," she agreed, vaguely pleased that he was worried about her.

"Good, I'll be back when I'm back. I'll let myself in. You get a good night's sleep." He absently patted her on the shoulder and left.

Ann watched him disappear down the stairwell and then rushed to the front window in time to see him emerge from the house and get into a waiting cab. She heaved an anticlimatic sigh as the red taillights disappeared into the darkness. So much for her big evening. But it didn't have to be a total loss, she thought suddenly, remembering the Jacuzzi. She could at least soak in his tub. From the sound of things, he would undoubtedly be gone for hours. She hurried toward the bathroom.

It was almost three hours later when the automatic lights went on in the study. Ann's eyes jerked open, and her heart began to race as her sleepy mind groped to get her bearings. A leering gargoyle peered down at her for a second before the room was plunged back into darkness. Marcus's bedroom. Muffled footsteps crossed the bedroom and entered the bath. Marcus's footsteps, she hoped, suddenly unsure.

She exhaled when Marcus was briefly illuminated in the dim light from the bathroom. Minutes later he was back and Ann watched with sleepy bemusement as he flung off his shirt, unzipped his pants and stepped out of them. But instead of lying down, he sat on the edge of the bed, his shoulders bowed, his hands dangling between his spread legs. He looked so desolate, so alone, that she couldn't remain silent.

"Marcus," she whispered into the darkness, "what's wrong?"

"Go back to sleep, Ann." His voice sounded old and infinitely tired.

Her concern for him overrode her normal reticence and she reached out, turned on the night-light and then touched his chilled shoulder. "Please, Marcus, what's wrong?"

"The bastard won," he said thickly. He turned, and her heart constricted at the naked pain filling his eyes. Instinctively she reached for him, offering the comfort of human contact. She half expected him to move away, but he didn't. He wrapped his arms around her and held her so tightly that it was almost painful, but she made no attempt to escape. He nestled his chin in her hair and rocked her back and forth as if what drove him wouldn't let him be still.

"What bastard?" she asked.

"Death." His voice chilled her. "I don't normally get involved in direct patient care, but she was the daughter of a friend of mine. Five years old—" his voice broke "—with big chocolate-brown eyes, glossy black curls and her whole life in front of her. Her pediatrician found the leukemia last year during a routine checkup. I really thought we could beat it, but it suddenly spread like wildfire. All my years and years of work, and it didn't do a damn bit of good. I might as well have been a witch doctor with beads and a rattle for all the difference I made. She was so young, so damned young!"

Ann held him tightly as if she could absorb and share some of the pain ripping him apart.

"Why? Why did it have to happen?"

"I don't even know all the questions, Marcus, let alone the answers," she said sadly, continuing to hold him, until finally, toward dawn he slipped into a restless sleep. For a long time she simply lay there, taking pleasure from watching his face, relaxed in sleep.

There were unexpected depths to Marcus Blackmore, she realized. As absentminded as he was, she would have thought that emotion wouldn't touch him very deeply, but it had. Not only touched, but savagely wounded. He cared and cared very intensively about some things. He was a complex personality, and she found herself wanting to get to know him better. An impulse she was quick to deride. She had no time to clutter up her life with personal relationships that would encroach on her mental energy.

She'd let things cool off during the two weeks he was in Boston, and probably by the time he returned, she'd be hard-pressed to remember exactly what it was she'd liked so much about him—besides his food. A rueful smile curved her lips. Cautiously she eased herself out of bed, dressed and let herself out of the house. In two weeks, he'd be a dim memory.

7

"YOU LOOK WORSE than I feel, Serendipity." Ann peered worriedly at the small white mouse. He was lying stretched out on the bottom of his cage, his minute pink tongue hanging out and his eyes closed. At the sound of her voice, his nose twitched dispiritedly.

"It must be over a hundred degrees in here." She tugged her sweat-dampened T-shirt away from her sticky body. "And the weatherman isn't predicting a break in the heat wave, handsome." She repositioned her one fan so that it was blowing directly on the mouse, but he didn't seem to notice the difference.

Ann sighed and picked up her book, but for once her beloved Greek failed to hold her interest. It was too hot to read, she told herself, refusing to acknowledge the extent of the lost, restless feeling that Marcus's trip to Boston had caused. Of course she missed him, she conceded. He was her friend. Her very good friend. A vivid memory of their last kiss bubbled to the forefront of her mind. It was only natural that she'd miss him. He was the only adult that she really talked to. At least in any depth or about anything other than superficialities. Even Peggy's conversation was limited to what Tom thought and what her kids did. Marcus filled a very real gap in her life. A gap that she'd barely been aware of until she'd gone out with him.

Over the past two weeks, she'd caught herself saving events from her days and tidbits from her reading to share with him, only to have her spirits drop when she remembered that he wasn't there. He was in Boston. She found her newly discovered impulse to share her thoughts and impressions very disconcerting. Never before had she wanted to do so. She'd always been a very self-contained person. But now, at twenty-seven, with Marcus, Ann had discovered the truth to the old saying that a pleasure shared was a pleasure doubled. To have him suddenly leave town was very disappointing.

An unconscious smile lit her face as her thoughts lingered on Marcus. They had a lot in common despite all their differences. And they were going to have even more once she got him reading. Her glance strayed to the paperback sitting on her bureau. She'd picked it up at the bookstore last Saturday on her bimonthly trip. A trip that had unexpectedly lost much of its appeal. Instead of concentrating on her selections, she'd kept seeing Marcus's dark head bent over the stacks of books. She'd even gone into the romance room and sat on the box of books that she'd shared with him. It was when she actually found herself fingering the historical novel he'd been reading that she'd taken herself firmly in hand. Missing a friend was one thing, mooning over him like a groupie was quite another.

"Drat the man!" She resolutely turned her attention to the book.

Fifteen minutes later, Ann was still staring at the middle of the same page, when there was a loud knocking on her door. She frowned, wondering who it was. No one ever visited her. It was probably someone selling something. She turned a page, deciding to ignore it. A feat that quickly took on gargantuan proportions as the pounding intensified. She threw down her book in disgust and stalked to the door, flinging it open.

"Quit that!" she snapped. "I . . . Marcus!" Hungrily her eyes traced the familiar lines of his face. No, not so familiar, she studied him uncertainly. His eyes were narrowed, his lips firmly pressed together and his jaw was clenched. He was furious about something.

"Why the hell haven't you got a phone!" He strode into her room and she automatically gave ground, although she wasn't sure that talking to him in his present mood was a good idea.

"I tried to call you when I got to Boston and the operator told me that you didn't have a phone!" he accused. "I thought everyone had a phone."

"It's not the first time you've been wrong, friend," she said mildly, relishing the thought that he'd actually tried to get in touch with her.

"Why haven't you got one?"

"What for?" She shrugged. "I'm rarely here to get calls."

"You shouldn't be here now," he said, the taut lines of his face beginning to smooth out. "At four on a Friday afternoon, you should be working at work."

"I did some overtime last week for a sick colleague and personnel gave me today off in exchange."

"Mmm." He glanced around the small room. "You call this place an apartment!" He was back to being furious.

"Why not?" She sank down in the room's one chair. "You call that storage shed for a construction company of yours a house."

"At least it's air-conditioned, and there's room to turn around in it," he retorted.

"I don't entertain people, and between work and school I'm not here that much myself except to sleep. Although, if it makes you happy, I will admit that I covet your air-conditioning. But next year, once I get a real job, we'll be able to afford some."

"We?" Marcus's bright blue eyes demanded an answer.

"Serendipity and I." She gestured toward the cage.

He frowned as he caught sight of the mouse. "Good Lord, do you still have that thing?"

"It's only been four weeks."

"Has it? Somehow it seems much longer," he murmured, leaving Ann to wonder exactly what he'd meant.

He opened the cage and picked up Serendipity, frowning as the mouse's tiny legs hung limply over his strong brown fingers.

"He's just a little hot." Ann's voice asked for reassurance, which she didn't get.

"To the point of heat prostration." He rubbed behind the mouse's ears with a gentle fingertip. "Really, Ann, when you kidnap someone, you have a certain responsibility to them."

"Maybe I could sneak him into the library." She'd barely heard his crack. "It's air-conditioned and open till ten."

"Considering his track record in public places . . ." Marcus's voice trailed away significantly, and she cringed at the memory of the diner.

"You and this repellent rodent—" he carefully placed the dispirited animal back in the cage "—had better come home with me until the heat wave's over."

Go home with him? Ann stared blankly at Marcus while she examined his words. Go home with him? Live with him in a house that only had one bed? A rising tide of excitement shortened her breath.

It was a bad idea. She knew she was playing with fire, and she was going to get burned when he suddenly forgot her existence. But she wasn't looking for a permanent relationship, she argued with herself. That didn't fit into her plans for years yet. And she was tired of living in a vacuum while waiting for the future to arrive. What was wrong with enriching the present? And living with Marcus would enrich it. He could enhance her present, exasperate her sense of order and stir up her deepest emotions, all without seeming to make the slightest effort.

For the first time in a long time, she felt vitally alive and full of pleasure at the thought of what the present offered. That feeling couldn't be wrong. She ruthlessly overroad the tiny voice in her mind urging caution. For once she intended to enjoy what she actually had, instead of looking forward to what she might someday have.

Marcus switched off the fan, picked up the cage and glanced around the room. "Do you want to bring anything?"

"A couple of changes of clothes." A sense of rightness engulfed her as she gave voice to her intentions. "The heat wave might not break for several days."

"Bring enough for the rest of the summer," he ordered. "It'll just get hot again. Where's your suitcase?"

"I don't have one. Nobody invites *me* to Boston," she added defensively at his incredulous look.

"You can come with me next time I go," he offered. "What about a sack?"

"I have an old box I can use." She pulled it out from under her narrow bed. She dumped its contents on the chair and hastily began packing her clothes into it, wishing she had a more elaborate wardrobe, one containing silk and lace underwear and slinky nighties. She sighed and flung in a plain cotton bra. Someday, she promised herself, but the promise brought no comfort. She wanted to be sexy and feminine now, not in the nebulous future.

"Anything else?" Marcus cut short her thoughts.

"Just my books." She dropped them on top of her clothes. "And yours." She added the paperback she'd gotten him.

"Not more science fiction?" He looked apprehensive.

"No science fiction, no angels, no ravishments. And no bodies," she hurriedly inserted when he opened his mouth.

"I don't know why Faulkner made such a big impression on you," he said mildly.

"On me?" Ann sputtered. "You're the one that drags that blasted body into every conversation."

He smiled complacently at her. "Not every one. You brought it up this time."

She closed her eyes, counted to three, opened them and tried again. "Trust me, you'll like this book."

"Oh, I trust you implicitly, but that's not to say I believe you."

She had no idea what she was supposed to make of that, so she didn't respond.

"Here, you take the cage, and I'll carry the box," Marcus instructed.

"Poor little creature," Ann encouraged Serendipity.

"You shouldn't get so attached to him," Marcus said seriously. "White mice don't live all that long. You ought to get another pet."

"I always wanted a dog like Lassie when I was a kid." She held the door open for him and then locked it behind them. "But my father changed jobs every couple of months, so we tended to move a lot."

"Tough," Marcus sympathized.

"Oh, it had its moments. As a kid I found sneaking out of apartments in the middle of the night one step ahead of eviction notices rather exciting." Deliberately changing the subject, she called, "Watch out for the stairs. They're a little rickety." She didn't want his pity.

"They're damned unsafe is what they are! Don't worry, we'll be home in ten minutes."

Actually, it was closer to fifteen by the time the taxi had deposited them in front of Marcus's brownstone.

"Unlock the door, would you?" He gestured with the box he was carrying. "The keys are in my right front pocket."

"Sure." Ann slipped her hand into the pocket of his gray slacks. Her fingers brushed against the hard muscles of his thigh, and a tingling shot up her arm. She quickly found his key ring amidst the change and pulled it out, unable to resist the impulse to allow her fingertips to linger as they trailed over his flesh. She glanced down at the keys and flexed her hand to dispel the lingering feel of him. "Which one is it?"

"The green one. I'll have to have another one made for you."

"That'd be nice," she responded cautiously. He was talking as if she was going to be a permanent fixture in his household, she thought, wondering just how permanent any woman would ever be to Marcus. At least she'd be harder to forget if she was actually sharing his home. The undeniable fact cheered her.

She unlocked the front door and flung it open, experiencing exquisite pleasure when the chill air rushed out to engulf them. She followed him inside, relocked the door and automatically headed up the stairs with Marcus right behind her. She was almost to the third floor when the magnitude of what she was doing hit her and panic set in. She didn't have the vaguest idea how to handle this situation. Should she act like a guest invited for the weekend or was something more personal called for? And if so, how personal? She clenched the handrail in frantic indecision.

"Are you dizzy!" Marcus demanded sharply.

"Umm...no...I...ah..." She took a deep breath and determinedly blanked her worries out of her mind. She'd wait and see how he played it and take her cue from him. "I was simply thinking and momentarily forgot where I was," she lied.

"Oh." He had no trouble relating to her excuse.

They reached the top floor and Marcus casually dropped her box onto the leather sofa, frowning at her flushed face.

"It wouldn't be a bad idea if you were to drink lots of liquids this afternoon. There's Coke in the refrigerator on the ground floor. And don't put that mouse in front of an air-conditioning vent, or he'll come down with pneumonia." He turned and started down the stairs. "I'll bring home dinner."

Ann frowned and leaned over the railing. "Where are you going?"

"To the lab. I was on my way there when I stopped to see you." He continued down the stairs.

So much for worrying about how to act. She grinned ruefully. Somehow being dumped in his house like a stray package hadn't been what she'd had in mind. It was rather anticlimactic.

"Well, friend." She studied Serendipity, who was beginning to look a little more alert in the cool air. "It looks like it's just you and I. Where would you like your cage to sit?" She scanned the huge room, her eyes lingering on Marcus's oversize desk. The banana peel was still there, she noted with disgust, resisting the impulse to dispose of it.

She wandered into the bedroom and looked around, finally deciding that the bureau top was the only practical choice for the cage. She carefully placed the piles of books covering it on the floor and then dusted its scarred surface with a handful of Kleenex.

"Now what?" she asked Serendipity, who twitched his nose disinterestedly. "Should I unpack and make myself at home, or should I wait for Marcus to offer me a drawer?"

Serendipity chattered happily as he began to poke around the bottom of his cage.

"You're right." Ann nodded emphatically. "He'd never notice that my clothes were waiting to be unpacked. He'd probably simply pile more books on them."

She opened the bottom drawer to find a specimen bottle filled with the most revolting-looking thing she'd ever seen. "Yuck!" She hastily slammed the drawer closed. No way was she sharing space with that monstrosity.

She'd use her box as a drawer and put it in the closet, she decided, then cautiously opened the door and peeked in. Knowing Marcus, she might find anything in there. What she found was the biggest closet she'd ever seen. No wonder he'd been so disparaging about her tiny apartment. His *closet* was almost as big. She set her box under a rack of his shirts, then curiously opened the door in the far wall, gasping at the blast of hot air that poured down the plain wooden stairs behind it.

The attic, she surmised, making her way up the steep steps. She was panting by the time she reached the top. The heat was overpowering. She took a quick glance around the enclosed area. It was littered with boxes, an old steamer trunk and several dilapidated pieces of furniture. She found Marcus's rejected computer leaning drunkenly against the brick chimney that rose through the center of the room. Determined to ask him if she could use it, she retreated down the stairs. It was much too hot to explore the attic.

She decided to get something to drink from the kitchen. On her way, she paused to take a closer look at the second level. There were two complete baths, each with whirlpool tubs, separate shower stalls and double sinks. She ran her fingers over the white Corian vanity top in the bathroom off the hallway. Marcus certainly hadn't spared any expense. From what she could make of the few framed-in walls, there would eventually be a huge master bedroom with its own bath as well as three other large bedrooms and one tiny one. A nursery?

She wondered if he had still been married when he'd bought this house. Perhaps that was why there were so many bedrooms. It was a line of reasoning she wasn't eager to explore, so she headed down to the first floor.

Ann passed through what was undoubtedly meant to be the living room, then a small dining room, a very large family room, and finally entered the kitchen. She looked around in appreciation. It was gorgeous. Wallpapered with bright yellow flowers on a white background, the room looked like something out of a home-decorating magazine. It even had a center cooking island with a breakfast bar at one end. But no stools, she noted with resignation. She opened the refrigerator, shuddering slightly at the containers filling the top shelves. Heaven only knew what they held.

She hastily grabbed a can of Coke and closed the door. If she were going to survive around Marcus, she was going to have to learn not to look too closely at things.

She suddenly yawned as exhaustion began to catch up with her. Between the overpowering heat and her loneliness, she hadn't been sleeping well for over a week. She'd lie down for half an hour, she decided, heading for the stairs.

Ann stirred under the thick comforter as the feather-light touch of firm lips brushed hers with tingling strokes. "Mmm?" she murmured sleepily, raising her head in an attempt to intensify the sensation, but the caress remained tantalizingly elusive. Lifting her lids, she found herself looking into the deep blue of Marcus's eyes. She stared, fascinated by the prisms of light that seemed to be dancing across his irises. She watched them come closer, and her heavy eyelids slid shut again as his lips touched hers.

Ann felt the mattress give as he sat down next to her hips. He leaned over, placing his hands on the comforter on either side of her shoulders, effectively pinning her to the bed.

Marcus lightly outlined her lips with the tip of his tongue and a jolt of sensation speared through her body, dispelling the last, lingering remnants of sleep. She twisted her head slightly, opening her mouth beneath his, but he didn't follow up on the unspoken invitation. Instead he withdrew slightly and smiled down into her bemused eyes.

"You're looking much better." His forefinger gently traced her softly flushed cheekbone.

She yawned and nuzzled his calloused palm. "I was sleepy. What time is it?"

"Five-thirty. I brought dinner. You get up while I unwrap it." He stood up and walked toward the front room.

Ann eyed his retreating back with dismay. She didn't want to eat. She wanted to kiss him, really kiss him, not to continue those light teasing touches he'd given her. She wanted to yank him into bed and seduce him. But before she could seduce him, she needed to get his attention, and right at this moment his attention was firmly centered on his dinner.

She flung aside the blanket and sat up on the side of the bed, wishing that she had the confidence necessary to risk making emotional demands on him. But she didn't and she knew it.

"Did you fall asleep again?" Marcus stuck his head back into the room, and she hastily got to her feet, swaying slightly at the disoriented feeling that swept her.

He frowned thoughtfully at her. "We'll have to start you on some exercises to improve your coordination."

"There's nothing wrong with my coordination." She glanced around the floor, trying to remember where she'd left her shoes. The other room, she finally recalled. "Falling asleep in the middle of the day always makes me groggy," she told him around an enormous yawn, and then padded toward the living room.

In the doorway, she tripped over a stack of books that hadn't been there when she'd gone to sleep and landed on the floor with a thump.

"Definitely clumsy." Marcus picked her up, gently dropped her on the sofa and handed her an icy can of Coke and a monstrous sub.

Ann stared pointedly at the scattered books in the doorway. "I'll buy clumsy, but the question is who?"

"Are they in the way?" He opened the tab on his can, and she watched in fascination as he tossed it on his desk, where it sank without a trace into the litter.

"Why would you think that just because I tripped over them?"

"No problem." He smiled agreeably at her and, picking them up, shoved them under the sofa.

"Thanks," she sighed in defeat, and unwrapped her sandwich.

"I got you the one that included a little of everything," he explained as she studied the different meats and cheeses, trying to calculate what it had cost.

"You got a lot of everything." She began to munch.

"You don't like it?"

"Oh, no. I like it just fine. If you'll tell me how much it cost, I'll reimburse you." She dreaded what that was going to do to the perpetually precarious state of her finances.

"Why?" Marcus studied her from the depths of his over-stuffed chair. "I've been plying you with food since the first time I met you, and you never offered to pay before."

"I know." Ann frowned. "But this is different."

"How?"

"Well . . . Before, you invited me out."

"I invited you here."

"I know that." She paused, groping to explain a feeling that wasn't exactly rational. "If you start to buy all my food, then there's going to be a subtle shift in our relationship. In effect I'll become your pensioner. I couldn't be contributing, I'd merely be taking. Taking your hospitality, your food, your air-conditioning. Oh, hell!" She grimaced. "I'm not explaining this very well."

"Well enough." Marcus looked thoughtful. "But when all's said and done, all we're talking about is money."

Ann smiled sadly, remembering the bitter harangues she'd endured from her ex-husband on the subject of "only money" every time her tuition payments had come due at the university.

"Believe me, Marcus, money only becomes irrelevant when you've got more than you need."

"Are you trying to tell me that you want our relationship to be split fifty-fifty financially?" he asked incredulously.

"Yes, ideally." She ground to a halt under Marcus's disbelieving stare. She knew she was explaining it badly. Mainly because it wasn't too clear in her own mind. The only thing she was certain of was that being financially dependent on Steve had proved a disaster, and she wasn't willing to subject the frail tendrils that bound her and Marcus together to those same dangers.

"That's the damnedest thing I've ever heard!" He glared at her. "You don't measure human relationships in terms of dollars and cents. And, even if you could, no relationship is static. Sometimes one partner needs to draw more than he's giving. Are you saying that you will only give exactly fifty percent and never any more no matter what your partner's needs happen to be at that moment?"

"No, of course not," Ann said tiredly. "Can't you see, Marcus, I don't mind giving. It's constantly being the taker that bothers me. What very quickly happens is that gratitude turns to resentment and, finally, bitterness." She spoke from experience.

"Your problem is that you're looking at this strictly in monetary terms, and I don't need money. But there are a few things you could contribute that I'd really appreciate."

"Oh?" She eyed him warily. If he even intimated that she go to bed with him as payment, she'd walk out of here and never come back!

"Uh-huh." He paused to devour a quarter of his sandwich. "Believe it or not, I could use a little help around here."

"A little?" she chided, her taut body relaxing. She should have known better. Marcus might have developed absent-mindedness into an art form, but he wasn't insensitive. Neither was he crude.

"Yes." Her sarcasm sailed right over his head. "Actually, I get tired of eating out, and sometimes I have fantasies about chocolate chip cookies hot from the oven." His eyes took on a faraway look. "And I never seem to remember to pick up the laundry."

"What you need is a—" Ann broke off in horror at what she'd almost blurted out. Marcus was liable to think that she was angling for the job of wife. And she wasn't. She didn't want to be anyone's wife. Not for years yet. Besides, she thought soberly, he'd already tried a wife, and obviously it hadn't worked out.

He finished her sentence for her. "Combination home manager and chef. How about if you take over the cooking and the laundry as your contribution?"

"Agreed." She nodded happily. He wasn't just creating a job for her. He really did need some help. Help that she was capable of providing. And would actually enjoy doing. She loved to cook and, while the same couldn't be said about the laundry, she could wash his when she did her own.

"Fine, finish your dinner and we'll go."

"Go where?"

"For groceries, so you can make some chocolate chip cookies and perhaps some brownies with thick chocolate icing, or maybe a coffee cake."

"I'll need a cookbook," she warned.

"Oh, I have one. My mother gave it to me the last time she visited. It's called *The Joy of Cooking*, but it's a lie. Cooking is not a joy. It's a disaster. And not only that but the brownies burned."

"I can imagine," she said truthfully, having no trouble picturing him putting something in the oven and promptly forgetting it. "But what about a grocery list?"

"We don't need a list. We need everything," he said seriously.

"Speaking of everything—" she recalled her foray into his refrigerator "—I know this is your house, but if I'm going to do the cooking, the horror show goes."

"Horror show?" He looked blank.

"Those slimy things entombed in jars in the refrigerator. They give me the willies."

"That's what comes of reading too much fiction," he scoffed. "They can't hurt you."

"Maybe—" she was clearly unconvinced "and maybe one of them contains a virulent plague that hasn't been discovered yet." She warmed to her theme. "Maybe even smallpox."

"No, we don't have any smallpox virus at this lab," he said seriously.

"What do you mean 'at this lab'?" She stared at him. "I was just kidding. Everyone knows that smallpox is extinct."

"True, but we still keep the virus alive."

"Do you mean to tell me that right now, in some lab there's active smallpox virus?" she demanded incredulously.

"Of course." He seemed puzzled by her outrage.

"But . . ." She stopped, took a deep breath, and continued. "We seem to have wandered rather far from the point. You can have your choice. Either your refrigerator contains milk and eggs and you get chocolate chip cookies, or it contains specimens and you eat out. I'm sorry to be unreasonable," she lied perfunctorily.

He sighed. "Don't worry about it. I think that women have a gene that predisposes them to dislike specimens in the refrigerator. Lucy used to come unglued every time she came across a tissue culture."

Lucy again. What had she been doing sharing his refrigerator?

"Actually, there's a simple solution. There's a refrigerator in the basement that I use for soft drinks. I could take that for my specimens, and you could use the one in the kitchen for cooking."

"Sounds good to me." She rewrapped the remainder of her sandwich. "I'll finish this later."

"If you're done, let's move the specimens and then go grocery shopping."

"I'll hold the doors and you move the specimens."

"Whatever. Come on." Marcus hustled her down the stairs.

As they passed the second floor, Ann was unable to resist the impulse to probe.

"You have a lot of bedrooms."

"Mmmm. But not as many as there were. They were all tiny, like cells."

"What made you decide on five bedrooms?" she asked curiously.

"Four," he corrected her. "That little room next to the master bedroom is a dressing room, although why on earth he thinks that anyone needs a separate room simply to get dressed . . ."

"He?" Ann pounced on the pronoun.

"The architect who redesigned the interior. He said four bedrooms would be best, considering bearing walls and all."

So it hadn't been his wife who'd designed it. She felt inexplicably cheered by the thought as she clattered down the bare oak stairs after him.

While Marcus removed his containers from the refrigerator, Ann busied herself opening cabinet doors. She found no food, but there was an impressive display of cooking utensils. She eyed a cylindrical bread pan with pleasure. She could hardly wait to get started.

"Get the basement door, would you?" He nodded toward the door in the far wall and she hurriedly opened it, barely noticing when the lights automatically turned on. She pressed herself against the wall, avoiding any contact with the containers he was carrying.

"Come on," he ordered. "I'll need you to open the refrigerator downstairs."

"Coming." She trailed along behind him at a safe distance.

8

"GOOD LORD!" Ann halted in amazement at the bottom of the stairs. The area bore no relationship to her idea of a basement. Paneled in warm, golden pine, it had been finished as a huge recreation room, almost the size of the entire house. The refrigerator that Marcus had referred to was built into a very professional-looking bar. A bar with four bar stools. Her eyes lit up. All she had to do was move two of them up to the kitchen and they could sit down to eat, she planned.

"Marcus—" her curiosity got the better of her "—why did you remodel the basement before the main living area?"

"Because while the carpenters were working down here, they weren't pestering me upstairs. Unfortunately, they finished in record time."

"They certainly did a superlative job." She glanced across what seemed to be acres of thick, honey-colored carpeting. There was no other furniture in the room except for a full-size pool table situated under an exquisitely beautiful Tiffany lamp.

"That lamp shade is gorgeous. Where did you ever find it?"

Marcus stopped arranging his containers in the refrigerator and glanced at it. "I didn't," he said absently.

"Who did?" she asked, wondering if this were yet another legacy of the elusive Lucy.

"That decorator." He smiled suddenly; he had figured out how to fit everything in. "But I got rid of her."

"Why? She did a beautiful job down here." Ann wandered over to where six very thick canvas mats were lying on the floor.

"Because I don't like surprises."

"She didn't ask you first?" Ann queried sceptically.

"Well, she said she had," he admitted. "But I don't remember it."

Ann tried to swallow the grin teasing her lips, but it broke through. She didn't have the slightest doubt that the poor decorator had caught him in an engrossed mood, and Marcus had simply agreed to everything without really hearing her. He was lucky that the woman had been competent, or there was no telling what he could have wound up with.

"It isn't funny," he complained. "What on earth am I supposed to do with a sauna or a bar or that thing." He waved toward the pool table.

"You've got a working sauna?"

"So the decorator said." He began stacking the Coke he'd taken out of the bar refrigerator. "But I've never tried it. I don't have time to sit and parboil myself."

"Do you mind if I do?"

"Only if I'm here. Saunas can be dangerous if misused."

"Most things can," she commented, then wandered over to the thick mats, wondering what they were for. They looked like the mats used for tumbling in her high school gym class. She slipped off her shoes and stepped onto a mate.

"Marcus, what do you use these for?"

"Workouts. I have a friend who practices karate with me. Once we whip you into some kind of basic shape, I'll teach you the fundamentals of self-defense."

"Thanks, but I'm not into the martial arts."

"You should at least know how to defend yourself. What would you do if you were attacked some night on your way home from work?"

"Scream," she answered flippantly, refusing to face the frightening possibility. She knew the danger of being out on New York City streets at midnight.

Ann watched enthralled as the light splintered through the colored glass of the Tiffany lamp shade, painting rainbows on the mat. There was a seal of some sort designed into the glass, she realized. She tilted her head to one side, trying to read the Latin inscription and then gasped in surprise as Marcus's large hand suddenly covered her mouth and his heavily muscled forearm closed around her upper body, pinning her to his hard chest. Her feet were dangling four inches off the floor.

"I didn't hear the scream," he said calmly, and she felt the words reverberate through his chest wall.

"What's your second line of defense?" he mocked.

Ann was annoyed, almost angry. She was perfectly aware of how vulnerable she was. She didn't need him to emphasize it. It would serve him right if she gave him a good swift kick in the shins. Not that she'd do much damage in her bare feet. Maybe, she should nip his palm to teach him a lesson. She squinted down at the hand covering the lower part of her face. It smelled faintly of soap with a very faint overlay of something astringent. She shut her eyes and breathed deeply trying to identify the smell, but the warmth from his hand was warming her cheek, eroding her concentration.

Tentatively, she tried to open her mouth, but Marcus increased the pressure of his hand to the point that she couldn't. Beginning to get genuinely angry now, she twisted in his hold only to find that his arm was a steel band.

She silently swore at how easily he managed to thwart her. It would have to be a kick, she decided. She swung her leg back, and he pinned her foot between his calves. Finally admitting defeat, she allowed her body to go slack and immediately found herself free.

"Still think you don't need some instruction in self-defense?" Marcus gave her a smug smile that absolutely infuriated her.

"Brute strength never proved anything!" she said hotly. Of all the self-satisfied males!

"It proves who's stronger," he retorted. "You couldn't fend off a prepubescent mugger."

"Could, too!" Ann retorted, immediately regretting her words. She'd sounded like a petulant five-year-old. She took a deep breath and tried to become the logical, rational adult she knew herself to be.

"Your demonstration proves absolutely nothing because you took me by surprise. I wasn't on guard—my friends rarely attack me," she said pointedly.

"All right." Marcus kicked off his shoes and stood on the mat in front of her, his body lightly balanced on the balls of his large feet.

"All right, what?" She eyed him uncertainly. "You're admitting that I'm right?"

"I'm admitting that you have a point, although I can't believe one of your friends hasn't attacked you before now, as infuriating as you are."

"Me?" Ann sputtered. "You're the one who's acting like something out of a Bruce Lee movie."

"Who's he?"

"He's . . . Oh, never mind. Just tell me why we're standing here."

"I'm giving you a chance to prove your point," he replied with a reasonableness she mistrusted. "You said that you didn't defend yourself because I took you by surprise. So now you are expecting an attack, defend yourself."

"Defend myself?" Her eyes lingered on the intimidating breadth of his shoulders. "You mean, when I foil your attack, you'll drop the subject?"

"Uh-huh." He nodded. "And, when I win, you'll let me give you some lessons in self-defense."

"You ought to give lessons in sheer stubbornness," she said exasperated.

"Is it agreed?" Marcus was relentless.

"Yes," she conceded, watching him warily, planning a strategy. She'd once read an article that had advocated delivering a sharp kick to the assailant's groin. Her eyes involuntarily dropped to his flat stomach, lingering on the masculine shape of him. No, definitely not. She didn't want to hurt him, she just wanted to shut him up.

She couldn't out-muscle him, and she wouldn't hurt him. That left guile. She'd trick him and then run. That should prove her point.

Her eyes traveled down his legs. She vaguely remembered a movie in which the villain had put his leg between the hero's and twisted, throwing the hero to the ground. And the beauty of that play would be that she didn't have to actually bring him to the floor. All she needed to do was to tip him off balance long enough to give herself a running start.

She glanced up to find Marcus watching her with a casual interest that put her on her mettle. He didn't expect any opposition. She'd show him.

Taking a deep breath, Ann lunged forward, but that was the only thing that went as she'd planned. Without quite understanding how it happened, she found herself lying on her back with Marcus astride her, his knees pinning her arms to her sides.

"How about best two out of three?" She smiled sheepishly at him.

"You aren't in a good position to negotiate," he pointed out.

Ann jerked suddenly in an attempt to shake him off, but he didn't budge. The vise of his legs tightened slightly.

"Game's over, Marcus." A breathless quality tinged her voice.

"But not the forfeit." Relaxing his grip, he gave her a slow, sensual smile that made her shift restlessly under the impact of it.

"Forfeit?" she whispered, her attention caught by the hot glowing depths swirling in his eyes.

"Hmmm, but I haven't quite decided just what I'll take." His fingertips traced down the center of her forehead and over the tip of her nose. "Such a small little nose, to lead you into so much trouble."

"I thought the expression was leading with your chin," she retorted.

"I was thinking more along the lines of a nose for trouble," he said laughingly, continuing his tactile exploration. First, tracing her eyebrows, then trailing over her cheekbones and down along her jawline. Her eyelids slid shut, and he tenderly brushed her lashes before moving down to outline her lips.

Ann expelled her breath on a long sigh when he ran his thumb over the uneven line of her bottom teeth. Her tongue brushed his skin, and she savored the slightly salty taste. She arched restively and suddenly became aware of the hard male shape of him. Forcing open heavy eyelids, she saw he was as affected by her as she was by him. The knowledge lent her confidence.

"Marcus, I want you to kiss me."

"Not as much as I want to, my inept little combatant." His voice sounded almost loving, but before she could fully analyze that, his mouth closed over hers and she forgot everything but scorching ardor.

She twisted restlessly. She wanted more than to merely be the recipient of his lovemaking. She wanted to share it. To explore the supple texture of his skin. She moaned in frustration when Marcus didn't seem to notice her desire to be free, and he drank the sound from her lips.

Finally he released her and, sitting beside her, pulled Ann up between his strongly muscled thighs. His hands delved under her T-shirt to cradle her breasts through the thin cotton of her bra. The heat from his calloused palms warmed the pliant flesh, and they swelled in anticipation.

She pressed against his hands, instinctively seeking to intensify the feeling. She gasped as he began to nuzzle the sensitive skin behind her ear. The tip of his tongue flicked over the fine hairs on the back of her neck and she twisted in his arms, barely noticing when her shirt fluttered to the floor.

"You're so beautiful," Marcus murmured. "So exquisitely perfect." His hands reverently cupped her breasts and he palmed her aching nipples, watching them grow taut beneath his ministrations.

Ann threaded her fingers through his silky black hair, her hands clenching as his mouth suddenly closed over the distended tip of her right breast. He held it lightly in his teeth as his tongue slowly rasped over the tight bud.

Ann began to tremble, and the tremors intensified as his hot mouth began to gently tug. Slowly he lowered her pliant body onto the mat. Pausing only to strip off his shirt, he covered her chest with his. He slowly rubbed back and forth, and a sob of pleasurable anguish shook her.

"So beautiful," Marcus's hoarse words fed her escalating desire. "Just let it happen, my lovely. Let go and I'll take care of everything."

"Marcus!" She clutched his broad shoulders, giving herself up entirely to the passion spiraling through her. "Marcus, I...you..." Her words escaped in a disoriented staccato.

She protested when Marcus's mouth left her breast to trail down her rib cage. A fever pitch of excitement engulfed her when he reached the elastic waistband of her shorts and slowly began to pull them down. His caressing lips followed. She lifted her hips while he drew the shorts down over her legs.

"Like velvet and satin." Marcus's husky voice stroked her passion higher, sending it out of control when he lightly scraped his short nails over the soft swell of her stomach. His hand slipped lower, between her legs. Her response was instinctive. There was no rational thought involved. No consideration of what he might think of her actions. She was the essence of feminine desire with but one purpose. Union with Marcus.

"Marcus, I want you. Now!"

"Not yet," he said, his voice husky. "First, you have to need me as badly as I need you." His long fingers began to probe the dampening heart of her.

"I don't believe the way I feel," she gasped.

"That's right, my lovely," he encouraged her. "Give yourself up to it." He began to trace erotic designs on the satiny skin of her inner thighs, heightening the tension that gripped her.

"I never knew..." She lifted her hips against his hand in unconscious demand. "Make love to me, Marcus," she pleaded. "Please, I want —"

"Exactly what I want, my precious one." He swiftly stood and stripped off his slacks, negligently tossing them aside. Ann stared up at him through passion-drugged eyes, glorying in the vibrant masculine force of him.

He quickly dropped down beside her, covering her body with his and slipping between her legs. Eagerly she welcomed him, her breath catching as she felt the taut heat of him probing her softness. She waited, every muscle of her body locked in desperate anticipation. A joyful cry escaped her as he entered her body.

His large hands gripped her hips, holding her tightly to him as he began to move deep within her, seemingly intent on impressing himself on the very essence of her soul. Frantically, she clung to his shoulders and then the thin thread holding her tethered to earth snapped, hurtling her into a magical kingdom.

Ann sighed in contentment as she heard Marcus's thick shout of satisfaction. She didn't want to move, ever. She sank into the warm, voluptuous clouds shrouding her mind. Dimly, she felt herself floating, a replete smile on her lips.

"WAKE UP, ANN." The command was accompanied by a gentle shake of her shoulder.

She muttered nastily and burrowed deeper into the thick depth of the down pillow. She didn't want to wake up. She pulled the quilt up over her ears. It was so lovely under the covers with the air-conditioning chilling her small nose. Nevertheless, she was beginning to surface through the layers of sleep that held her captive.

When she did finally come fully awake, she found herself staring into Marcus's blue eyes. Impatient blue eyes, she registered.

Ann squeezed her eyelids closed as memory came flooding back. She'd gone to bed with Marcus. If you could describe what had happened by such a prosaic term. It had been a revelation to her. Like seeing a color television after always having viewed black and white. Basically familiar sensations had developed depths, tones and textures she'd never imagined they held. She felt as if she'd just discovered the secret of creation. But that could hardly hold true for Marcus. She suddenly felt embarrassed. What should she say to him?

Hello, lover? She silently tried the words, listening to them echo into the farthest recesses of her mind. She didn't have the nerve. She froze as a warm finger suddenly pulled up her eyelid and peered into her eye.

"Are you in there?"

His ridiculous query effectively shattered the panicky uncertainty that had held her captive. Their having made love hadn't changed Marcus. He was behaving normally. At least, normally for him.

"And you have a medical degree?" She grinned at him and started to stretch, hastily retreating under the covers when she realized that she was totally nude. His attitude may have made her feel more relaxed, but not that relaxed!

"I didn't bother to bring your clothes up," he explained. "Just you."

"You carried me up three flights of stairs!" She suddenly realized how she'd gotten into his bed.

"Unlike some people—" he gave her a significant stare "—I'm in excellent shape and you're nothing but a bundle of skin and bones. Of course—" he paused meditatively "—you do have some interesting protrusions. I especially liked..."

"Thank you." Ann hastily interrupted, faint red staining her cheeks. She didn't think that she was ready to deal with his opinion of her figure. "But you still shouldn't have carried me up all those stairs."

"Well, you wouldn't wake up, and I could hardly leave you lying there on the mat. Think of what my friend would say when he came to practice karate and discovered you."

"Don't be fatuous." She scooted over toward the center of the bed as he sat down beside her hips. "I only needed a short nap."

"You needed a lot more than that." Marcus flicked the tip of her nose with a gentle forefinger. "It's nine-thirty."

"But it can't be!" She glanced at the sunlight pouring through the windows. "It's light outside."

"Nine-thirty the next morning," he enlightened her. "I considered trying harder to wake you, but you were sleeping so peacefully that I didn't have the heart."

"Sorry. What with this heat wave, I've been having trouble sleeping lately," she told him. It was half true. "And it's so lovely and cool in here. But I meant to be better company."

"I didn't invite you to entertain me."

The obvious question hovered on the tip of her tongue, but she bit it back. Knowing Marcus, if she asked he'd tell her and she didn't really want to know. She preferred uncertainty tinged with hope to the plain, unvarnished truth.

"But I am sorry I fell asleep," she repeated. "We were going to go to the grocery store."

"That's okay. I went myself. I unpacked the perishables, but I left the rest for you to do."

"Thank you." She smiled at him, grateful that he'd remembered. She wouldn't have been the least bit surprised to have found puddles of melted ice cream and soured milk on his kitchen floor.

"Speaking of food, that's why I finally woke you. I'm going down to the deli to get some bagels for breakfast. What kind do you like?"

"Onion, salt or garlic. Failing that, whatever they've got."

"I'll have garlic, too," he announced with a slow smile. After studying her soft pink lips for lingering moments, he bent over and lightly kissed the tip of her nose. Then to her intense disappointment, he stood up.

Ann's eyes followed his movement, took in the soft denim of his jeans and the thin cotton of his yellow knit shirt. Warmth sparked to life deep within her, her mind readily supplying the image of what was under the shirt. She pressed the palms of her hands into the soft cotton sheets, trying to control her urges. Who cared about eating when they could be doing something so much more fulfilling. But she lacked the self-confidence to make demands on their newly realigned relationship.

His calm voice recalled her. "What are your plans for the day?"

"Plans?" Her eyes lingered on his lean face, and a melting sensation grew in her abdomen as she considered what he'd say if she were to reply truthfully.

"As groggy as you are, I think you'd best include an afternoon nap."

"Lovely," she murmured dreamily, and then flushed. She resolutely banished her half-awake daydreams and got a grip on herself. Clearing her throat, she continued, "All I have to do is the washing. Where's the nearest Laundromat?"

"About half a mile away, but you can use the washer and dryer in the basement."

"If you have a washer and dryer, why do you use the Laundromat?"

"Too temperamental."

"I already know you're temperamental." She eyed him indulgently.

"Not me! The washer. When I tried to use it, I couldn't find a measuring cup, so I simply poured in the soap." He shuddered. "It was an even worse mess than the dishwasher."

"The dishwasher?"

"Hmm." He grimaced at the memory. "I didn't have any dishwasher detergent, so I used liquid dish soap."

"Dish soap!" Ann stared at him in disbelief.

"Soap's soap," he defended himself.

"What happened?"

"Soap suds. They came pouring out. Up over the cabinets. Down over the floor. And after all that, the cup wasn't even clean. It was sticky."

"Cup?"

"The coffee cup I was trying to wash."

"You ran an entire load for one coffee cup!"

"A dishwasher is supposed to clean dishes, and I had a dirty cup."

"Of course you did." She said with a sigh. "Never mind about the dishes. I'll take care of them."

"Thanks. But if I helped with the laundry, would you have time to bake some chocolate chip cookies?" A hopeful light illuminated his eyes, and a feeling of tenderness filled her.

She hastily refused his offer. "Laundry's no problem with a washer and dryer right in the house. I'll have lots of time to bake this afternoon."

"Great." He beamed at her. "I'll be back in fifteen minutes with the bagels."

Ann waited until the thud of his Adidas on the bare stairs died away before she tossed back the covers and stood up. She knew it was ridiculous to feel shy in front of him, but she couldn't help it. The habits of a lifetime were not so easily thrown off.

She hurried into the closet, extracted fresh clothes from her box and went into the bath. A quick shower and she'd feel a little less unsettled, she assured herself. And if Marcus was coming back in fifteen minutes, she had to hurry.

She wanted to drag two bar stools up from the basement so they could eat in the kitchen.

Ann finished her shower in record time and rushed downstairs. She felt marvelous. Invigorated, like a child on December the twenty-fourth. As if her life had suddenly become worth living *now*, instead of sometime in the future.

She burst into the kitchen and came to a surprised halt as she almost fell over a grocery sack. She gasped, staring around in disbelief. There were sacks everywhere. They covered the floor, littered the countertops and even filled the sink. She picked the sack up off one of the stove's burners and looked around for a place to put it. There wasn't one. She set it back down. Marcus hadn't just visited the grocery store, he'd brought a large portion of it home with him.

She opened the refrigerator, despairing at the incredible jumble of items fighting for space. Shaking her head, she began to straighten them, hoping to have the job finished by the time he returned. She didn't want him to think that she was criticizing his efforts.

Two hours later, she'd not only put away the groceries, she'd started the laundry, cleaned the bathroom, made the bed, vacuumed the whole top floor and brewed a pot of coffee in the brand-new drip percolator she'd discovered in the back of the pantry.

She poured herself a cup of coffee and climbed onto the bar stool. Marcus had clearly said he was going to the corner for bagels. Lurid visions of his having been caught in the middle of a holdup and being shot flashed through her mind.

Don't be ridiculous, she told herself. Knowing Marcus, he'd probably forgotten that he'd gone out for bagels and gone on to the institute. It could be hours before he came back. Days even. Ann felt depressed in the face of the reality. But at least she wouldn't starve.

Never had she seen so much food in her life. Even the freezer was filled. He'd done a very thorough job; she gave credit where it was due. She would have expected him to have forgotten half the essentials of a kitchen, but he hadn't. Nor had he forgotten a vast number of nonessentials. Although what he expected her to do with ground turmeric, she didn't know. And as for the pickled pig's feet . . . she shuddered.

Damn! Where was he? Briefly she considered calling the institute to see if he was there, but sanity prevailed. She was Marcus's guest, not his keeper. Even if he could have used one, she thought acidly. If she began to smother him, she would quickly find herself back home. Being his lover didn't give her the right to make demands. If they were really lovers. She took a thoughtful sip of her coffee. What actually made two people lovers, she wondered. Not simply going to bed together. That much she was sure of.

She and her ex-husband had never been lovers. Friends, yes. Friends with nothing more than a shared background in common. Now, with the wisdom of hindsight, she knew that what she'd felt for her ex-husband had simply been friendship compounded by her own compulsive desire to have a settled home and to really belong somewhere.

But there was a lot more than that to her feelings for Marcus. She liked his sense of humor, the way he gave his total attention to what he was doing, his thoughtfulness, his gentleness and the way he'd understood that her pride demanded she contribute something to their living arrangements. And underlying her liking was a deep respect for the man himself. But did all that make them lovers?

The rattle of the front door interrupted her unsettling thoughts, and she ran suddenly damp palms down her thighs. Her heartbeat accelerated. Marcus was back. She jumped up and headed toward the front door.

9

MARCUS WAS STANDING just inside the front door. The brilliant August sunshine pouring through the irregularly shaped antique glass of the fanlight had splintered into a rainbow of colors. It streamed down over his dark head engulfing him in a halo of light. He looked like an angel. Ann blinked to shatter the illusion. Marcus might be many things, but he wasn't an angel. He had much too earthy an attitude for that appellation.

"Hi," she offered.

"I have a surprise for you." He beamed at her.

"A surprise?" she said cautiously, her eyes automatically checking his hands. They were empty. Wherever he'd been, it hadn't included a trip to the deli.

He moved aside and pointed behind him with a gesture reminiscent of a magician conjuring a rabbit out of a hat.

Ann frowned and looked again. No, not a rabbit. A dog, and not a very prepossessing specimen at that. It was about twelve inches tall and fourteen inches long with a short stubby tail tucked between its legs. It was covered with dark gray fur that, with the exception of a small black nose, totally obscured his features.

"A dog?" She took a step toward it, and it scuttled back behind Marcus's legs.

"Uh-huh." Marcus reached down and picked him up. "He was supposed to be a collie."

"What happened?" she asked with a smile. "Did someone explain genetics to him?"

Marcus sat down on the stairs, holding the shivering animal on his lap. Ann sank down beside them.

"You said you always wanted a collie," he explained, and she stared at him in surprise. She had said it, and she'd meant it, too, but for Marcus to have actually remembered it . . .

"So, when I passed a pet shop this morning, I thought I'd buy you a collie." He paused to gently tug the still-shivering animal's ears. "You did?" she probed.

"Hmm, but the store didn't sell dogs. They go in for the more exotic types of pets. They had the most incredible python." His eyes took on a faraway look.

"Python as in snake?" She was unable to suppress a shudder of horror.

"A beautiful specimen. Eight feet long. But they eat mice, you know," he said regretfully. "So I decided not to get him."

Ann breathed a silent prayer to whichever guardian angel had been looking out for her this morning.

"Anyway," he continued, "the clerk in the pet store told me where to find the nearest animal shelter, and I decided to go over and see if they had a collie."

"I take it they didn't?" She glanced down at the small quivering animal.

"Actually they had several. But on our way through the shelter to see them, I found him." He nodded down at the dog in his lap. "And today was the seventh day he'd been there."

"What does that have to do with it?"

"It means I couldn't leave him." Marcus's eyes were frankly pleading for her to understand.

"You know, Marcus—" she frowned at him "—I'm catching all the words, but I'm not getting any meaning. I still don't know what the fact that he'd been there for seven days has to do with anything."

"They only hold them seven days and, if they aren't adopted, then they dispose of them to make room for the new arrivals."

"You mean . . ." Her hand instinctively covered the small furry head.

Marcus nodded. "So, you see, I couldn't leave him."

"Of course you couldn't," she assured him. "And, anyway, he's a very nice little puppy."

"He's not a puppy. He's mostly a miniature poodle about a year and a half old."

"If he's that old, doesn't he belong to somebody?"

"He did. To an elderly lady who had to go into a nursing home. She couldn't find anyone who was willing to take him so she took him to the animal shelter in the hope that they'd have better luck. But the woman there said that people want puppies." He glanced at her.

"Not me," she responded to the question in his eyes. "Puppies chew slippers and make messes on floors." She frowned suspiciously at the dog.

"Oh, he's housebroken. Mrs. Dalrymple says he has delightful manners."

"Mrs. Dalrymple? The woman at the shelter?"

"No, the lady who owned him. She'd been calling the shelter every day to see if they'd placed him yet. She was very worried. That's what took so long. I had to go over to the nursing home and tell her that he'd have a good home here."

Ann looked up at Marcus and a feeling of incredible tenderness swept over her. Not only had he remembered that she'd wanted a collie and tried to find her one, but he'd also taken the time to visit an old lady he'd never met to assure her that her pet would be well looked after.

"Marcus Blackmore, you are definitely one of the Lord's better attempts at creation." She leaned over and gently kissed his firm mouth. Her lips instinctively clung, and she pressed slightly as a tingling warmth spread from the contact. Regretfully she moved back as a fetid odor filled her nostrils. She eyed the small beast, who seemed to be trying to burrow under Marcus's shirt.

"I think our first order of business had better be to give him a bath." She wrinkled her nose expressively. "You might not have noticed it, but your protégé smells like something you put on the garden in the springtime."

"The whole shelter smelled like that." Marcus started up the stairs.

"What's his name?" Ann asked curiously as she followed him.

"Jefferson."

"Jefferson!" she repeated incredulously. "What ever happened to the traditional poodle names like Pierre or Jacques or Fifi?"

"Or Toulouse Lautrec?" Marcus added dryly.

"Point taken," she giggled. "Jefferson it is. He'll be much better than a collie anyway. Collies are working dogs that need a lot of exercise." And a lot of food, she added silently. She'd find it much cheaper to feed Jefferson once she was back in her own apartment. The thought momentarily depressed her, but she refused to dwell on it. She wasn't going to poison the present by worrying about the future. She was going to savor her association with Marcus. Savor and cherish it. Not overwhelm it with doubts and might have beens.

"Exercise won't be a problem," he claimed. "We'll simply throw him out in the backyard."

"What backyard?" She paused on the second-floor landing and Marcus halted a step above her.

"The yard out back," he explained. "It's as wide as the house and about fifty feet deep with an eight-foot-high brick wall around it. Where are you going?" he called after her as she began to pick her way through the building material littering the floor.

"I want to see this yard. There aren't any windows facing that way on the top floor."

She pressed her forehead up against the pane in the back bedroom and looked down. She blinked and looked again. There wasn't so much as a blade of grass to be seen. Every inch of ground was covered with an incredible litter of boards, bricks and hunks of dissolving plaster. It was an unbelievable mess.

"You can't put Jefferson out there," she objected.

"Why not?" Marcus leaned over her shoulder and looked, too. For a brief second Ann forgot her indignation as the warmth from his large body engulfed her. Fortunately for her peace of mind, the fetid odor surrounding the dog also intruded.

"So that's what they did with all those walls they tore out," he said mildly.

"That's all you've got to say?" she demanded incredulously. "You could have rats out there!"

"Rats?" Marcus suddenly looked thoughtful. "Maybe I should get that python after all. He could . . ."

Ann searched his bright blue eyes for a twinkle. To her dismay, there wasn't one. He was serious. "Listen to me, Marcus Blackmore," she spoke slowly and distinctly. "No snake. No matter what. Besides," she added, "you couldn't really have rats out there, or the health department would have been around before now."

"Probably," he conceded. "Rats congregate where there's food, and there's no food in the yard."

"A good point." She hurried back toward the stairs, sorry she'd ever mentioned the mess. That snake had obviously made a deep impression on him and, if she weren't careful, she was going to have all eight feet of it on her hands. She shuddered at the very thought.

Deciding that the tub would be better than the sink, she ran two inches of warm water in it and then turned to Marcus.

"What should we bathe him with?" She studied the shaking animal who was trying to hide under Marcus's chin.

"A mild, unscented soap. We don't want to irritate his skin." He nodded toward the linen closet. "There should be some plain castile soap on the top shelf. And get the mineral oil and an unused eyedropper out of the medicine cabinet."

Ann quickly found the soap, unwrapped it and dropped it into the water. Then she opened the medicine chest, her eyes widening in surprise at the neatly ordered rows of precisely labeled bottles. Obviously his casualness did not extend to medicine. She extracted the mineral oil and opened the package containing the eyedropper, then looked inquiringly at Marcus.

"What am I supposed to do with it?"

"Put two drops of the oil in each of his eyes."

She looked down at the unhappy bundle in Marcus's arms. "Why would I want to do that?"

"To protect them. Even though that soap's mild, it can still irritate, and we're bound to splash some suds in."

"True," she reluctantly conceded. She filled the medicine dropper and then stared down at the dog. "I can't see his eyes."

"Just push his hair back."

Ann did, and found herself looking into a pair of fathomless black orbs. She swallowed nervously and held the eyedropper up.

Jefferson whined piteously at her movement.

"I can't do it, Marcus. I might hurt him."

"You won't hurt him," he replied patiently.

"Maybe, and maybe the bottle was labeled wrong. Maybe it really contains something that could hurt him."

"Taste it," he suggested dryly.

"Taste it?"

"And see if it contains poison."

"But then I'd be dead," she stalled.

"You're going to be very shortly anyway, if you don't get on with it!"

"I'm getting, I'm getting." She cleared her throat and, ignoring the anguished expression in Jefferson's eyes, raised the dropper, determined to do her part. Marcus was right. It was for the dog's own good.

"Now what?" he asked in resignation as her hand remained suspended in midair.

"He closed his eyes, and I'm waiting for him to open them," she replied seriously.

"Oh, for crying out loud! Here, you hold him." He handed her the limp bundle of shivering wool. "I'll do it."

"Be careful," she said earnestly.

"Why don't you simply close your eyes until it's over?" he suggested, a sardonic expression on his face.

"I am not a chicken." She forced herself to watch while he competently placed exactly two drops of oil in each eye. "It's just that I get to thinking about all the things that could go wrong."

"You've got too much imagination for your own good." He plucked the dog out of her arms and placed him in the tub. "I'll hold and you wash."

"Right." Determined to redeem herself, she grabbed the bar of soap and quickly worked up a heavy lather, trying to ignore the dog's pitiful yowls, which were beginning to unnerve her.

"Just a minute more, boy. All I have to do is to rinse you off." She grabbed the portable shower head from the side of the tub and flipped it on, not noticing in her haste that it was pointing up instead of down. An error Marcus immediately became aware of as the spray soaked his shoulder.

"Ann! Watch what you're doing!"

"Sorry," she muttered, becoming thoroughly rattled. In her haste to correct the problem, she turned it too far and managed to catch Marcus's chin and upper chest.

"Sorry," she muttered again, trying not to notice the way the water was dripping off him. "Do you want me to dry you?"

"No thanks, I shudder to think what you might accomplish with something as lethal as a towel. Just finish."

"Right." She managed at last to get the spray aimed in the right direction and hurriedly rinsed the dog.

"Where's a towel," she asked, trying not to look at Marcus. The front of his shirt was damply plastered to his chest, emphasizing its muscular width and giving rise to a whole series of emotions that she tried to tell herself were entirely inappropriate to the situation.

"Hold him and I'll get one," he said, and she lightly put her hands around the bedraggled animal.

Too lightly. As if sensing that she wasn't a force to be reckoned with, Jefferson jerked out of her grasp and scrambled up the side of the tub.

"Jefferson, come back here!" Ann lunged for him, managing to tumble into the tub.

"Woman, you have got to be the clumsiest person I have ever met." Marcus scooped up the dog, who was dashing for the bathroom door, and he enveloped him in a large cream bath sheet.

"I am not clumsy!" She splashed the filthy water she was sitting in in disgust. "I was trying to catch him."

"Why didn't you simply hold on to him in the first place?" He began to rub the small animal dry.

"I was," she snapped. She climbed out of the tub, her clothes streaming dirty water and her temper badly frayed. She peered balefully at the small head peeping out from the folds of the towel.

Jefferson, obviously feeling that he'd gotten the better of her, gave a satisfied smirk.

"If you'd been holding him properly, he wouldn't have escaped and you wouldn't be a mess," Marcus calmly pointed out.

"And if you dare to say one more word, I'll . . ." She stamped her foot in anger; it squished damply.

"Oh, I wouldn't dream of saying I told you so." His eyes laughed at her. "Even though I did." He gently dried Jefferson's ear. "There, beastie."

"I think I'll put him in the closet to finish drying off. I can easily close the air-conditioning vent in there so that he won't get a chill."

"Good idea." She pulled her soaking T-shirt away from her damp breasts, waiting for Marcus to leave before she took a shower. Despite the intimacy that they'd shared the night before, she couldn't force herself to calmly strip off her clothes in front of him.

"I'd better take a couple of towels for him to snuggle up in." Marcus carelessly pulled two ivory-colored towels out of the closet, not seeming to notice Ann's discomfort. Cradling the dog on his right hip, he flung the towels over his shoulder and left.

Ann expelled her breath on a long shuddering sigh as the door swung shut behind him. She swiftly yanked off her wet clothes and flung them into the sink. Turning on the shower, she stepped into its warm spray and began to thoroughly soap her slender limbs as she tried to put this morning's events into some kind of perspective. Perhaps Marcus had simply passed the pet shop and remembered what she'd said about always wanting a collie and decided to buy her one. But why? Why go to all that trouble? Especially when the pet store hadn't had a collie and he'd had to go chasing off to an animal shelter.

If Marcus was a normal person, she'd say that he'd done it to please her. But Marcus wasn't normal. The only thing that she was sure of was that she had somehow acquired a small dog.

"Eek!" Ann let out a startled squeak as the shower door suddenly swung open and Marcus slipped inside. She caught a quick glance of his broad chest before her gaze skittered downward, focusing on the way the shower droplets were splashing on the ceramic-tiled floor. She shivered when his hair-covered thighs brushed against her bare legs. His muscular arm encircled her waist and gently nudged her forward to give him more room.

She moistened her lips and watched in mesmerized fascination as his large hand reached around her and picked up the soap from the soap dish. She'd never shared a shower with a man in her life. It seemed so intimate. She contemplated pretending she was finished and getting out. It was as if Marcus was intent on indelibly stamping his presence on all areas of her life. As if he were showing her that their relationship encompassed every aspect of daily living, not just lovemaking.

"There," she said brightly, having decided to retreat. "I'm done."

"Not quite. You missed a spot here on your back," he observed.

"I . . ." Ann swallowed uncertainly as the tips of his fingers traced lightly over her shoulder blade.

"I'll help. Hold still."

I may never move again, she thought dreamily as the roughened palm of his hand began to gently massage her spine. She closed her eyes and arched her back into the caressing movement. Her breathing became more rapid as his wet fingertips slipped around her rib cage to glide slickly over her stomach. She jerked, slipping slightly, as one of his hands slid lower and drew her back against the cradle of his hips.

"Definitely the clumsiest lady of my acquaintance," he murmured.

"I'm not," she objected on a strangled gasp. She could feel his hard-muscled frame down her entire length, and her thoughts were scattering like dry leaves in the wind.

Marcus nuzzled the soft skin under her ear and Ann squirmed. His teeth lightly nipped her earlobe and his arm pulled her tighter into his embrace, making her devastatingly aware of the effect she was having on him. The knowledge gave her the courage to rub her hand over his thigh. The result was instantaneous. He swung her around, crushing her pliant frame against his.

A tremendous rush of emotion—a compound of passion, wonder, joy and expectancy—surged through her, feeding her self-confidence. Marcus wanted her. The knowledge was clearly written in the hot glow in his eyes. She leaned forward and lightly touched his lips with hers.

"I want to kiss you," she whispered. "I want to . . ." She paused, too shy to actually put her desire into words.

"To kiss every inch of your glorious body," he concluded. The reverent tone of his voice momentarily con-

fused her, and she lost her train of thought completely when
he pulled her toward him.

He lightly touched the rapidly beating pulse point in her
neck with the tip of his tongue before moving to explore the
hollow at the base of her throat. Her breath was coming in
short, shallow gasps, making her acutely aware of the scent
of him. The lingering remnants of his after-shave mingled
with the faintly astringent aroma of the pine soap that covered them both.

Losing interest in her neck, his lips began a leisurely exploration of the shape of her collarbone. "You taste so
sweet." Marcus's husky words fell into the well of her desire, forcing it up over the rim of her self-control. She
clenched her jaw as excitement coiled the muscles of her
abdomen, and her fingers clutched his hard shoulders,
trying to draw him closer.

"Marcus, let's go into the bedroom." She ran her hand
distractedly over his broad chest.

"But we don't need a bed," he murmured. "Variety is the
spice of life."

"You know some of the most interesting clichés." Her
words escaped on a soft sigh. "But I don't see . . ."

"Don't you, my lovely?" His voice was threaded with
sparkling promise.

Ann jerked as his hand splayed over the slight swell of her
stomach. Marcus flexed his fingers, and their hardened tips
sank into her silken skin. Her eyes narrowed to slits, and she
savored the torrent of feeling cascading through her. She
could see tiny prisms of color, the brilliant light from the
overhead fixture splintering the dancing sparks of water into
thousands of incandescent rainbows.

How apt, she thought dreamily. Marcus had added so
much color to the drabness of her monotonous world. She
gasped as his probing hands suddenly encircled her. Brac-

ing himself against the ceramic wall of the shower, he cupped her hips in his hands, then pulled her upward along the length of his water-slicked skin. Her eyes widened, and her heartbeat began a stacatto rhythm as she felt the hard, throbbing force of his masculinity.

"Marcus!" she gasped, then froze when she realized exactly what he intended.

"It's all right, my lovely," he crooned. "Relax."

"We'll drown," she protested, vaguely shocked by what he was doing even as her body instinctively pressed closer.

"Trust me, Ann."

"Yes." The word trembled in the air between them like a vow. Of course she trusted him, she thought. Marcus would never hurt her. She felt her doubts fade away. Obeying his silent command, she wrapped her legs around his waist and clutched his neck as he slowly positioned his body at the portal of her femininity.

A shimmering surge of urgency gripped her at the tantalizing contact, and she intuitively tried to deepen their intimacy.

"That's right," Marcus encouraged her, surging upward at the same time his hands forced her hips downwards. A starburst of pleasure so intense it was almost a physical pain engulfed her.

Ann arched her back, forcing herself yet closer to him. Her eyelids slid closed, weighted down by the desire that ricocheted through her mind.

"Move with me, my precious one." His guiding hands began to ease her body into an erotic rhythm. A rhythm that was amplified by the hot shards of water beating on her burning skin.

Her hunger grew, becoming a seemingly insatiable demand as her whole world narrowed to the pulsating force of him. Their location as well as the precariousness of her position had no place in her thoughts. The only reality was Marcus and her all-encompassing need imperiously demanding fulfillment. A fulfillment that, when it came, left her oblivious to everything but the exquisite pleasure rippling through her. Even Marcus's shout of satisfaction failed to penetrate her total absorption. Slowly she drifted back to awareness to find herself being carried into the bedroom.

"We'll get the sheets all wet," Ann murmured perfunctorily, as he dropped her onto the bed. She snuggled her head into his shoulder, deeply inhaling the clean, male scent of his damp skin. She stretched, amazed at the spark of desire that briefly flared when her leg brushed his. It seemed inconceivable that she could want him so soon after what had just happened.

Her dreamy reverie was cut short by her stomach's loud growl. She flushed, embarrassed. Growling stomachs did not go with tender love scenes.

"Hungry?" Marcus peered down at the soft, flat planes of her abdomen.

Ann clenched her fists into the tumbled sheets, but she resisted the impulse to dive under the covers. She knew that feeling embarrassed at having him look at her was ridiculous, considering what they'd just shared. But it was one thing to glory in his interest in her body while in the throes of passion and quite another to do it in the cold light of day.

Marcus slanted a brief look up into her face and flashed a wicked grin. "Not only clumsy, but shy?" he teased gently.

"I am not clumsy." She was too honest to try to deny the rest.

"And starving," he added as her stomach rumbled again. He glanced at the digital clock beside the bed. "You should have eaten more breakfast."

"I should have . . ." she sputtered.

"Breakfast is the most important meal of the day," he added earnestly, when she simply stared at him.

The wretched man was serious! He was actually giving her a lecture on the importance of eating breakfast when the reason she'd missed hers was because she'd been waiting for him to return with the bagels. The humor of the situation suddenly struck her, and a reluctant smile teased her lips.

"I'll remember that," she said gravely.

"I'll remind you," he offered, and it was all she could do to turn her laughter into a strangled cough. He'd remind her! Now she'd heard everything.

"Are you chilled?" He frowned at her quivering body.

"No, just hungry."

"Tell you what." He sat up and swung his legs over the side of the bed. Ann studied the outline of his muscles rippling beneath his supple skin. "It's after one," he continued. "You don't want to waste time fixing lunch when you're planning on making chocolate chip cookies this afternoon." He gave her a hopeful look.

"True," she agreed, pleased to be able to do something for him. Her pleasure mushroomed at the happy expression that lit his face. Marcus was such a complicated mixture of overwhelming intelligence, absentmindedness, thoughtfulness and just plain boyish enthusiasms. His personality would take her a lifetime to plumb. A lifetime she didn't have. But Marcus was the present. An enriching present that she wasn't going to spoil by worrying about the future. She'd done enough of that already.

"So I'll run down to the deli and get some bagels for lunch, okay?"

"Good idea," she replied cautiously, wondering if she'd actually get them this time.

"What kind do you like?"

"Onion, salt and garlic," she repeated, waiting for him to remember that they'd already held this conversation earlier. To her fascinated amusement, he didn't. He merely slipped on clean clothes and, with an absent smile and a murmured "I'll be back in fifteen minutes," left.

I wonder what I'll get this time? she thought, listening to the sound of his receding footsteps. The memory of the snake popped into her mind and she shuddered, casting a protective glance at the sleeping Serendipity. No oversize garter snake was going to get its fangs into her white mouse. Or dog. The muted howls coming from the closet reminded her of Jefferson's presence and she untangled herself from the sheets and hastily pulled on shorts and a T-shirt before rescuing the still-damp animal from the closet.

"Well, my friend, you don't smell like the bottom of a rabbit hutch anymore. Now you smell like a wet wool sweater." She studied the small beast consideringly. "And you look like the before segment of a fabric softener commercial. Maybe I should have used some conditioner on you. Your hair, or whatever that stuff covering you is, is flying every which way."

A fact that didn't seem to bother him at all. He suddenly came to life, racing across the floor and down the stairs.

Ann took off after him. She caught up with him on the bedroom level, where he was busily sniffing a pile of discarded lumber. She hurried to pick him up, afraid that his manners might not prove equal to the occasion. Apparently he thought it was some kind of game, for he danced out of reach and, moving to yet another pile of trash, sat down and barked encouragingly at her.

Ann watched his fuzzy tail swish through the dust with resignation. His tiny mouth opened, and his pink tongue lolled out.

"You stay right where you are," she ordered, and began to slowly creep toward him, ending with a mad dash when he bounded up. She had almost reached him when a burning pain sliced through her and she came to a precipitous halt. Her right foot throbbed in agony and she looked down, swallowing uneasily at the sight of the bloodstained nail protruding from the top of her bare foot. That was her blood, her stunned mind registered. She'd actually stepped on a nail. A huge nail.

I'll never live down his dumb idea that I'm clumsy was her stunned reaction, followed swiftly by a half-formed plan to get the wound cleaned up and bandaged before Marcus returned.

It quickly became apparent that she couldn't. Her one attempt to yank her foot free convinced her to wait for help. There was a buzzing in her ears and she felt faint. A chill sweat broke out on her forehead, and she crouched over her injured foot, determined not to pass out and make a bad situation worse.

A cold nose brushed up against her bare leg, and she smiled weakly at the small dog.

"Maybe I should change your name to Nemesis, although I suppose it's unfair to blame you. I'm certainly old enough to watch where I'm going."

Jefferson thumped his tail encouragingly, and Ann coughed at the cloud of dust he raised.

She sighed in resignation. "We'll simply have to wait for Marcus," she groaned, and then a horrible thought occurred to her. Suppose he forgot he had gone out for bagels as he'd done this morning? Suppose he went over to the institute and didn't come back for hours? The buzzing in her ears increased, and she ducked her head toward the floor.

She'd wait twenty minutes and, if he hadn't returned, then she'd fix it herself. She was a responsible adult who was capable of managing her own problems, she encouraged herself. If only the problem wasn't covered with blood; she glanced down at the nail in despair.

Suddenly Jefferson began to bark and, scrambling over a pile of litter, took off down the stairs.

What on earth . . . Ann tilted her head to one side, trying to hear over his yapping.

"Ann?"

It was Marcus. A feeling of indescribable relief swept over her. Marcus was here. Everything would be all right.

"I'm on the bedroom floor. Could you come up, please?"

"What are you doing?" he asked as he walked toward her with Jefferson dancing around his feet.

"Umm . . . I . . ." She paused, trying to find a logical way to explain her accident. It was unnecessary. Marcus glanced down and saw the problem.

"What the hell did you do?"

"What does it look like I did?" she snapped. She needed help, not an inquisition.

"It looks like you ran true to form." He hunched down beside her and ran a gentle hand over her throbbing foot.

Ann opened her mouth to insist that she wasn't clumsy and then closed it. She could argue the point later from a more comfortable position.

"I tried to pull it out," she offered. "But it made me sick."

"Mmm." He probed and a whimper of pain escaped through her clenched teeth.

"I'll be right back." He stood up.

"Where are you going!" she wailed.

"To wash my hands and get something to help," he threw over his shoulder.

"Get what?" She was left with no choice but to wait.

He was back almost immediately.

"What's that?" She warily eyed the syringe he was holding.

"A numbing agent." He held the needle upright and squirted a droplet of the clear liquid into the air.

She shrank back. "I don't like needles."

"Believe me, Ann, you'd like feeling me pull that nail free even less. Now close your eyes. You'll feel a pinprick followed by a sensation of cold."

"I'll throw up," she threatened.

"Then I'll clean it up." He swiftly plunged the needle into her foot, and she gasped in dismay. But to her relief, it wasn't as bad as she'd feared.

Almost at once her foot began to lose feeling, and within five minutes, Marcus was able to remove the nail.

"You can look now," he said gently. "It's out."

Ann glanced down, gasped and hurriedly looked back up at him.

"Thank you. If you'd just help me to the bathroom, I'll put some disinfectant on it."

"They'll do that in the emergency room." He swept her up into his arms. "I called a cab when I was upstairs. It should be here by now." He started down the stairs.

"Emergency room! I'm not going to any hospital."

"Like hell you're not!" His flat voice was emphatic. "Puncture wounds are dangerous, and that one is one of the worst I've ever seen. It needs to be cleaned, and you'll need a tetanus shot."

"I had one," she insisted.

"When?"

"I don't remember exactly."

"Then you'll have another. People still die of lockjaw, even today."

"All right," she suddenly capitulated. "I'm sorry. I didn't mean to cause all this trouble," she apologized, swallowing an uncharacteristic desire to burst into tears. This wasn't turning out at all like she'd planned. She'd intended to be the perfect roommate and, instead, she was causing him all kinds of inconvenience. And not only that, but there was nothing even faintly romantic about stabbing herself with a nail. Who would have thought that, when she'd tried to convince him that she was a klutz, it would come true? She sniffed disconsolately.

"Don't snivel." His arms tightened comfortingly around her. "I'll hold your hand."

"THERE." Marcus gently lowered Ann onto the sofa and studied her pale face narrowly. "Why don't you take a nap? I don't like your color."

"Is there any?" She tried to make a joke of it. "I swear I could feel all the blood drain out of my face when that doctor cleaned the wound."

"Milk white with a tinge of gray." He ran a gentle finger down her cheek, and she smiled weakly at his comforting gesture. "Would you like something to drink?" he asked. "A cold Coke?"

Which was in the kitchen, two flights down, she thought. She couldn't let him wait on her. He'd very quickly begin to wish he'd never met her, let alone invited her home—if he didn't already. A panicky feeling shook her. She should go back to her apartment. At least until she had two good feet again. Maybe Marcus would keep Jefferson for a few days. Just until her foot healed enough so that she could negotiate her apartment stairs with a little more ease.

She put her doubts into words. "Actually, I think I'd like to go home."

"Why?" he demanded.

"Well . . ." She shrugged. "I didn't count on any of this."

"Me, neither, but knowing how clumsy you are, I suppose I should have been prepared for something."

"I am not clumsy!"

"Besides—" he ignored her protest "—you heard that doctor. You're to stay off that foot as much as possible for twenty-four hours. Not only that, but your apartment is like the inside of an oven, and the temperature is going up, not down."

She blurted out her real reason. "But I don't want to be a bother. I'm causing you all kinds of trouble."

"A few minor inconveniences, nothing astronomical. And you're a lot more fun to lift than my weights."

"That's nice of you to say, but . . ."

"Not particularly." He grinned wryly at her. "I'd be a pretty strange sort of man if I preferred holding a steel barbell to an armful of sexy woman."

The last two words echoed welcomingly in her ears. Did he really think that she was sexy? Her ex-husband hadn't. The thought momentarily chilled her, but she brushed it aside. Not all men were alike, and Marcus certainly made love to her as if he found it a pleasurable experience.

"So quit worrying. I'll go get us a couple of Cokes and check on what Jefferson's doing. What about lunch?" He paused at the top of the stairs. "A bagel heavy on the cream cheese and lox?"

"No, thank you." Ann swallowed uneasily, her queasy stomach revolted at the very thought of food.

"Later then." He disappeared from sight down the stairwell.

Ann leaned back and closed her eyes, feeling as if she'd completely lost control of things. Until Marcus had appeared on the scene, her life had been so orderly. Everything had been going exactly according to her carefully formulated plans. But now . . . She sighed. Now she felt as if she was no longer in complete command. That's because she wasn't truly living until she met Marcus, she answered herself. She was simply passing time in the present while wait ing for the future. There's always more danger in experiencing life than in simply observing it from the sidelines. Although this was one experience that she'd just as soon missed.

Ann yawned and slipped into a light sleep. She didn't notice when Marcus returned with their drinks, nor when he covered her with a blanket.

Two hours later, the hot throbbing in her foot bludgeoned the last remnants of sleep from her mind. She shifted restlessly, trying to find a comfortable position, but it proved impossible. The ache came from within, radiating up her shinbone.

She moistened her dry lips, feeling incredibly thirsty. She had to get something to drink. She glanced around the large room, immediately locating Marcus. He was bent over the huge pile of papers that littered his desk, reading something with absorbed interest. As she watched, he made a notation in the margin and flipped the page. Her eyes took on a covetous gleam when she noticed the unopened can of Coke on the edge of his desk. She swallowed again, and her eyes closed in anticipated pleasure at the very thought of the bubbly liquid.

She flung off the blanket and sat up, wincing as her injured foot hit the floor. Gamely, Ann got to her feet and hobbled across the room that had suddenly assumed the proportions of a football field. She reached for the can, losing her precarious balance when Jefferson popped out from underneath the desk. She hastily steadied herself and stole a quick glance at Marcus. He was still deep in whatever it was he was reading. Unwilling to admit even to herself that she wanted his attention, she took the soft drink and made her way back to the sofa, followed by the small dog.

She sank back down and opened the Coke, taking a long, satisfying drink of the lukewarm liquid. To her amusement

Jefferson jumped up beside her and eyed her soda long-ingly, clearly expecting a share.

"Dogs don't drink soda. And they don't sit on furniture, either," she told him sternly, feeling like a heartless brute when his small fuzzy ears dropped.

"And even if I wanted to give you some, I don't have a saucer, and you can't drink out of a can."

He whined in what seemed to be negation of the idea.

"Not on your life, buddy. No way am I going to share a can with a dog. But I guess you can stay on the sofa," she offered placatingly at his woebegone expression. He was clean enough, she decided, justifying her concession. And, anyway, Marcus wouldn't care. If he even noticed. She glanced tenderly at him. He was still deep in whatever it was that he was reading. The man had the most incredible powers of concentration she'd ever seen.

And you'd better concentrate on your FORTRAN les-son, she lectured herself. You've got a test on Tuesday. But she wouldn't be able to go to work on Monday, she sud-denly realized. She could study Monday night. So instead of doing something she had to do, she'd do something she wanted to do. She'd read that translation of *The Meno* by Rouse she'd found at the bookstore last week. She'd been wanting to compare his translation to her own ever since she'd discovered it.

Unfortunately, it wasn't the pleasure she'd anticipated. The pain in her foot made it impossible for her to concen-trate. Her discomfort filled her mind to the exclusion of everything else. Sighing, she closed her book and looked up to find Marcus staring at her.

She grimaced. "Sorry. I didn't mean to disturb you."

"You didn't. I finished the report. Is your foot painful?"

"A little," she lied, not wanting to sound like a com-plainer.

"A little in relation to what?" he asked dryly. "Having it amputated? I think you'd better take a couple of those painkillers they gave you. I'll get them." He stood up and stretched, and Ann watched as his muscles rippled beneath his thin shirt. Not even the pain seemed to dull her instinctive response to him.

"Wait here. I left them downstairs. I'll be right back."

"Where does he think I'll go?" Ann demanded of the dog sleeping at the end of the sofa. Jefferson didn't venture an opinion, merely contenting himself with a desultory wag of his stubby tail.

Marcus was back within minutes with her pills, an onion bagel lavishly spread with cream cheese and two more Cokes. "Here." He handed her the medicine, then opened a can and gave it to her. "Swallow them," he ordered, and Ann, unable to resist the promise of relief, did. "Now eat that," he gave her the bagel.

"Thanks, but . . ."

"Eat," he repeated. "You haven't had anything since last night."

Ann reluctantly took the plate. She wasn't in the least hungry. In fact, she still hadn't shaken her queasy feeling, and it was unthinkable that she get sick to her stomach and cause more trouble.

"If you eat your bagel, I'll fix you a hot fudge sundae with lots of whipped cream and chopped nuts," he coaxed. "It's great in the microwave."

"The ice cream?"

"No, the hot fudge."

Ann picked up her bagel and took a bite, determined not to appear temperamental. For some reason it was important to Marcus that she eat and, continuing to refuse, was making her sound like a prima donna.

He watched in satisfaction as she munched her way through the bagel.

"Would you like your sundae now?" he asked when she'd finished.

"No, I think I'll save it for later. But you know what I would like? That computer you dumped in the attic."

"Why would you want that thing?" Marcus looked at her in surprise.

"Because I'm going to pay you back for what you've done for me today."

"I was trying to help," he defended himself.

"I know that." She laughed. "That's why I'm going to do you the favor of organizing your data."

"It sounds more like revenge to me," he muttered darkly.

"Trust me. You'll like it."

"You said that about that book you gave me."

"Oh." Ann brightened. "I forgot. I bought you another variety of fiction. You can read it while I start keying your information in."

"But I was going to work on something else." He gazed longingly at his desk.

"Just for an hour? In case I need to ask you any questions."

"You can still ask me questions if I'm working."

"Marcus." She eyed him ruefully. "The archangel Gabriel and a heavenly host singing the hallelujah chorus couldn't get your attention once you start working."

"It's not that bad," he protested.

"It's not bad at all," she agreed. "In fact, if the truth were known, I wish I had your ability to shut out the world at will. It simply makes things rather awkward when someone wants to talk to you. So, if you'll just read my book for an hour, I'll be able to get a good start on getting your facts in."

"It ate my information the last time." He was clearly unconvinced.

"But I know what I'm doing," she persisted.

"All right," he capitulated. "But just for an hour."

"Thanks, you won't regret it," she called after him as he headed for the attic and the discarded computer.

Half an hour later, Ann had it set up and working. She pressed return and watched the bright green letters light the screen.

"This is a lovely machine," she enthused.

"That's a contradiction in terms," Marcus grumbled. "No computer is lovely. I wouldn't be surprised if they weren't being pushed on us by the Russians to cause dissension."

"Nah." Ann smiled at his self-righteous expression. "It's really part of the plot to fluoridate the water. Now, what should we input. You bought plenty of disks." She glanced at the three full boxes he'd set beside her.

"No, I didn't. They came with it. Tell you what, why don't you start sorting through some of the things on my desk." He picked up the nearest stack and handed it to her.

"Good idea." Ann brightened. She'd been wanting to get her hands on that mess since the first time she'd seen it. "I'll divide your work into categories, and then you can decide what to enter first."

She glanced over the top page that contained row upon row of figures, breathing a sigh of relief to find everything very clearly labeled. At least she wasn't going to have to cope with illegible scrawls.

"Why don't you start your new book while I begin this. It's called *Ten Little Indians*, and it's in my box of stuff in the closet." She ignored his disgruntled mutterings and started to shift through the stack.

Halfway down, she discovered some unopened mail. Curiously, she glanced at the postmarks. They were all three weeks old.

"Marcus? Marcus!"

He gave her a blank look over the top of the paperback, blinked and then focused on her inquiring features.

"What?"

"You have some mail here. Unopened," she added when he showed no interest. "It could be important."

"No," he seemed unconcerned. "If it was important, they'd contact me at the institute."

"You mean you aren't even going to open them!" she demanded in disbelief. She loved to get mail and rarely did, and here was Marcus who did get mail and he couldn't be bothered to even open it.

"You read it."

"But it's your mail!"

"So tell me what it says."

"All right." She opened the top one and glanced down at the signature. "It's from your mother."

"Hmm?" He looked up from the book. "What does she have to say?"

"Well." Ann skimmed the page. "She thanks you for your Christmas card and says that it was inspired to send it out in June instead of December. That way it didn't get lost in the shuffle with everyone else's. In June?" she asked, unable to resist.

"I bought them in October," he said defensively. "But they got misplaced, and I didn't find them until I was packing to leave California in June. I didn't know what else to do with them, so I just put them in the mail."

"I'll bet they were on your desk, weren't they?"

"Uh-huh. How'd you know?"

"An educated guess." She glanced ruefully at his heaping desk.

"What else does she say?"

"That your father's arthritis is much better this year, and she hopes you're planning on visiting during September." Sadness engulfed Ann at the thought of his leaving town again. She'd missed him so much when he'd been in Boston. She determinedly shook off the feeling and continued. "She ends by saying that if you don't write soon, she's going to file a missing-persons report on you with the NYPD."

"Mothers!" he snorted.

Ann studied him, curious about what kind of people had produced him. His mother's letter had seemed so normal.

"What's she like?" She heard herself ask, even though she knew that any information that intertwined her more deeply with Marcus's life was a mistake. Each tie that snapped when they parted would be one more tendril to ache.

"Oh, you know," he said carelessly. "Typical mother. Trying to run your life for you. Probably just like yours."

"No." A trace of bitterness crept into her voice. "Not like mine. Mine sends me a card on my birthday and at Christmas and in between times tries to pretend that I don't exist."

"Why?" Marcus gazed at her. "You're intelligent, personable, and very pretty. The type of daughter any parent would be proud to claim."

A glow warmed her at his words, which were all the more believable because of the dispassionate tone in which they'd been uttered. "Oh, it's not me personally. I'm simply the tangible reminder of her first marriage. One that she'd much rather forget. Not that I blame her," Ann said honestly. "My father was a womanizing con man."

"Was?"

"Yes. When I was fifteen he wrapped his car around a tree one night."

"I take it your mother remarried?"

"Two months after the funeral. To a widower with four little kids."

"That bothered you?"

"Not that she remarried or even that she did it so soon. It was the way she threw herself into becoming the perfect stepmother. I quickly became the odd man out."

"Rough," he sympathized.

"Oh, it wasn't that bad. She didn't try to palm me off on the state or anything like that. Anyway, it all happened a long time ago." Ann smiled brightly, already regretting her impulse to talk. "It's hardly relevant today."

"No," he agreed. "It's your mother's problem, not yours."

But it had become hers, she thought soberly. Because of her desire to belong somewhere, she'd rushed into marriage with Steve.

Marcus diverted her unhappy thoughts. "What other mail was there?"

"Let's see. This one's from Burton and Smythe."

"Burton," he elaborated. "He's my accountant. What does he want?"

"He says to please return some of his calls because you have to authorize an investment. That you've accumulated too much cash in your checking account."

"I knew there was something I meant to do."

"Call Burton?"

"No, play back my phone-answering machine."

"I think you'd be better off without it," Ann suggested seriously. "At least then people would know they hadn't contacted you, instead of thinking you were ignoring them."

"Why would anyone think I was ignoring them?"

"You mean, simply because you don't read their letters and disregard their calls?" she asked dryly.

"I'll get around to it. What's the last one?"

"Looks like an invitation to a wedding." Ann glanced at the thick cream vellum envelope. She slit it open and read the bronzed engraving. "No, it's an invitation to the christening of the son of Caleb and Lucy Bannister." Lucy, the name leaped out at her. Lucy wasn't all that common a name. Was it the same Lucy who had stocked his kitchen? Was she married and a new mother? Ann had to know.

"Is that the Lucy you've mentioned before?" She tried for a casual note.

"Uh-huh." Marcus flipped a page. "Good old Lucy."

Good old Lucy was not a threat, Ann thought happily, and then abruptly sobered having realized exactly what she was thinking. What was there to threaten in her relationship with Marcus? They were friends and hopefully lovers, but their relationship by its very nature had a time limit. A fact that suited them both. She ruthlessly silenced the totally unexpected doubts that bubbled through her mind.

"When is it? We'll have to go."

Ann's spirits rose at the way he automatically included her in the invitation, and she glanced down at the date.

"Not unless you've finally figured out time travel," she teased. "It was last Sunday."

"Want to do some more research?" He gave her a slow smile, and her stomach twisted at the sensuality in his voice. She shifted restlessly under the hot glow lighting the depths of his eyes. She managed to jar her foot. At her wince, Marcus's eyes narrowed.

"Give those capsules another half hour," he said. "By then it should be quite a bit better."

"It's not too bad. As long as I don't move it," she added under his disbelieving stare. "About this invitation, you really ought to send a gift."

"Even though I didn't go?"

"Especially since you didn't go," Ann stated emphatically. "If you've known Lucy for so long, her feelings were probably hurt."

"Not Lucy." Marcus went back to his mystery. "She knows me too well."

"She does?"

"Umm." He continued to read. "We used to be married."

Ann's eyes widened. Why hadn't she considered that before, she wondered, and then answered her own question. Because of the way he always spoke of Lucy—sort of absently, lovingly, as though she were a favorite sister. There were none of the bitter undertones of disappointed hopes that marred her recollections of her own marriage. What kind of relationship had Marcus and Lucy had? The question burned in her mind, but she couldn't figure out any way to ask without sounding as if she was probing into something that was none of her business.

Marcus's pleased voice cut into her thoughts. "I have it."

"Have what?"

"A christening gift. I'll name the virus I just discovered after him. It'll be different." He looked pleased with himself "Not like all those silver christening cups everyone else always brings."

"It'll definitely be different," she agreed, "but . . ."

"But what?"

"Well . . ." She searched for words. She didn't want to shatter his pleasure in his idea, but on the other hand, a *virus*. "It's a gift for posterity," she temporized. "And when he's an adult having a virus named after him would probably give him a real thrill." She kept her doubts firmly to herself. "But maybe we ought to include another gift, as well. For now. Something that would appeal to a little boy."

"There's that python at the pet shop. Boys like snakes. I liked snakes."

"You are not a specific from which to generalize," she said tartly. "You are unique."

"Thank you." Marcus grinned at her.

"I haven't decided if that's a compliment yet."

"Then I'll have to work harder to make you appreciate my qualities." The sensual light was back in his eyes. "Just as soon as you've recovered."

"Anyway," she doggedly returned to the original subject. "Lucy's son might someday like an eight-foot-long python, but I guarantee she won't."

"You could be right. I remember once when we were kids. I tried to get Lucy to hold a squashed garter snake I'd found by the side of the road while I dissected it. She didn't stop screaming for an hour." He shook his head in disgust. "Lucy has absolutely no spirit of scientific inquiry."

"Well, if we're choosing up sides, put me in with Lucy." Ann shuddered.

"It's not your fault. It's the conditioning women are exposed to from the cradle," he soothed, forgiving her magnanimously. "But you can overcome it."

"I don't want to overcome it," she said emphatically. "And I doubt if Lucy does, either. So scotch the snake."

"Then what'll we get him?"

"A toy," she decided. "We'll get him a toy."

"If you like." He went back to his book. "But I still like the snake."

Lucy owes me one, Ann thought, then returned to sorting through Marcus's papers. And so would Marcus once she got this all organized for him. She smiled, anticipating his pleasure once she'd finally managed to show him what a useful tool a computer could be.

ANN GLANCED at the digital clock on the microwave oven. Ten-fifteen. She sipped her coffee and debated calling a cab to take her to the doctor's office for her appointment to have her foot checked. If she did call one, she could sit here for another fifteen minutes and enjoy the unaccustomed luxury of having nothing to do. Normally at this time of the morning, she'd be dashing between classes. This morning she was relaxing in a silent house with the prospect of a whole day to do exactly as she pleased.

She smiled at the quiet that sat so lightly on her ears. She hadn't fully appreciated just how noisy her own apartment was until she'd moved in with Marcus. Absolutely no sounds filtered in from their neighbors on either side.

"And I hope none filters back." She glanced reprovingly at Jefferson who wagged his tail, refusing to take offense. "Trying to eat the mailman through the letter box is definitely unacceptable behavior. Not only that, but you scared the poor soul half to death."

Jefferson gave her a superior sniff and snuggled back up under the bar stool she was sitting on.

"Talking to you is like talking to Marcus," Ann complained. "I'm never quite sure whether or not I'm getting through."

She finished her coffee and wiggled her foot experimentally. Even after two days, it was still slightly sore, but she could easily walk on it. Maybe she ought to take the bus to the doctor's office and then take a cab back if her foot started aching. Suddenly Jefferson startled her by scrambling to his feet and racing for the front door, yapping at the top of his lungs.

"Good Lord, now what?" She hurried after him. He'd already permanently alienated the postal service this morning. That was enough for one day.

The second she heard the key turning in the lock, she knew it was Marcus.

"What are you doing home on a Monday morning?" she asked when the door opened.

Marcus bent down and rubbed Jefferson's back, then flung his briefcase on the stairs. It hit the fourth step, teetered on the edge and clattered down to the third.

Ann ignored it. "Why are you home?"

"To take you to your doctor's appointment," he replied. "Have you forgotten your checkup?"

She stared at him in openmouthed amazement. Marcus had actually remembered that the doctor had given her a follow-up appointment. And he'd remembered it before the event, not after. She searched his features for some visible sign to explain his unusual behavior, but he looked exactly the same. Could his memory have suddenly taken a turn for the better? Did this signal things to come?

"You did forget," he said, misinterpreting her dumbfounded silence. "Well, it doesn't matter. I've got a cab waiting. It shouldn't take very long."

It hadn't, thanks to Marcus. The office nurse had greeted him with all the enthusiasm of a teenybopper faced with a rock star. With a speech about appreciating how busy Dr. Blackmore was, she'd ushered them through the overflowing waiting room and into an examining room. Ann had felt guilty about skipping to the head of the line, but she knew that the nurse was right. Marcus was busy at the institute. Much too busy to have come with her.

Her physician had seemed as impressed with Marcus as his nurse had been, and Ann had felt curiously unsettled at their deferential treatment of him. It was as if her familiar

Marcus were slightly out of focus. A feeling that disippated once they left the office.

"If you were to drop me off at school, I could still catch half my classes," she suggested as they were getting into the cab.

"No." Marcus gave his home address to the bored-looking cabbie. "Weren't you listening to what the doctor said?"

"He's just being overly cautious. There is no way I'm going to miss another two days of school! And as for staying home from work for a whole week—" She broke off in annoyance at the idea.

"I've already told personnel you won't be in until next Monday at the earliest," he replied calmly. "That's what sick days are for," he continued in the face of her incredulous expression. "And the reason your foot feels so well at the moment is because you've been staying off it."

She hadn't had any other choice, what with Marcus watching her like a hawk. But she couldn't bring herself to object more strenuously. It had been a long time since anyone had fussed over her, and she was honest enough to admit that she liked the feeling of being cherished.

"But, Marcus, I'm used to being busy. What will I do with all that free time?"

"Read a book, take a nap . . ."

"I finished my last book yesterday, and I've had so much sleep lately that I could probably stay up all night and never notice it."

"Then play with that computer you're so enamored of."

"I've already keyed in all the information in that tiny, little stack you let me have." She gave him a meaningful, wistful look.

"Well, I guess you can finish sorting the reports on my desk," he agreed reluctantly. "But don't remove anything from the room. Promise?"

"Cross my heart," she swore hastily, eagerly planning how to make the maximum use of his moment of weakness.

"NICE SERENDIPITY." Ann absently rubbed his tiny chest with the eraser on her pencil. She frowned over the column of numbers on the paper in front of her. To her surprise, she had found that Marcus's work appeared to consist mainly of gathering seemingly endless rows of figures. She set the sheet to one side of the desk to be keyed into the computer later.

"You know, Serendipity, I hate to pass judgment, but to me Marcus's research seems about as interesting as my cleaning labs. He . . . stop eating my eraser!" She hastily pulled the pencil back and looked at the gnawed end. "You'll make yourself sick," she lectured him, but Serendipity was singularly unimpressed.

He stuck his nose between the bars of his cage and chattered protestingly at the loss of what he obviously considered a tasty snack.

"Here, try a dog biscuit instead." Ann shoved one into his cage. "Yes, you, too, beastie." She dropped one on the floor for Jefferson. "Although heaven knows you don't deserve a treat. You've got to stop trying to eat the mailman."

Jefferson cocked his head to one side, dropped the biscuit under Marcus's desk and in a flurry of frenzied yapping took off down the stairs.

"Speaking of antisocial behavior," Ann muttered, getting to her feet. Someone was probably at the door. Jefferson's hearing was absolutely uncanny. Sure enough, a second later, the muted chimes of the front doorbell rang.

She glanced at her watch before going to answer it. Nine-ten. The mailman had already come. And gone. She remembered the man's pithy comments on wild beasts. Marcus wasn't due home to take her to lunch until twelve-thirty. She brightened at the thought. So who did that leave?

She landed squarely on her injured foot and a sharp jabbing pain shot up her leg. It had been four days since the accident, and the foot only hurt if she happened to land directly on it. She hurriedly limped across the foyer, scooped up the barking dog and peered through the leaded glass windows beside the door.

There were eight men standing on her stoop, each carrying a variety of tools. Her displeased glance went to the curb, where a paneled truck and a pickup truck with the legend Anderson Construction Company emblazoned on their doors were parked. She studied the men carefully. They seemed harmless enough, she finally decided, flinging open the door.

"May I help you?" Ann cradled the growling Jefferson to her chest.

"You can if you're—" the man who appeared to be the leader checked the clipboard he was holding "—Ann Somerton?" He raised an inquiring eyebrow and she almost burst out laughing, remembering Marcus's abortive attempts.

"Yes, I am," she hastily answered at his impatient frown.

"Dr. Blackmore said you'd be here to let us in."

"Oh?"

"So do you suppose you could do it?"

"Do what?" she asked in confusion, trying to figure out what was going on.

"*Let us in.*" He enunciated the words very carefully. "Dr. Blackmore said you'd let us in so that we could begin work."

"Oh, of course." Ann hastily moved to one side and the men trooped in.

"Umm, exactly what is it you're going to do, Mr....?"

"Ed, just Ed. Finish up the house." He glanced around consideringly. "Like I told Dr. Blackmore when he called yesterday, with a full crew and seeing as how all the plumbing and most of the electrical work's done, we can have it finished in a couple of weeks. Three at the most. Of course, I didn't figure dodging bad-tempered dogs into the estimate." He glanced sourly at the growling Jefferson.

"He isn't..." Ann started to defend him and then smiled weakly when Jefferson snapped at the men. "I'll put him in the bedroom at the top of the house and shut the door," she promised.

"See that you do," Ed warned, and then motioned his crew into the living room.

Ann thoughtfully made her way upstairs. According to Ed, Marcus had called them yesterday. Why had he done that? Why would he suddenly call in the builders to finish remodeling when the house had been sitting like this for well over a year. It hadn't bothered him before. She dropped Jefferson onto the bed and went back into the sitting room, closing the door on his pathetic howls at having his freedom curtailed.

Ann sank down in the leather sofa and tried to weigh the situation logically. The only thing she was aware of that had changed between last week and today was that she'd injured herself on one of the many scrap heaps on the first two floors. Given Marcus's seemingly unshakable belief that she was hopelessly maladroit, he probably thought that it was simply a matter of time before she ran afoul of another piece of the builder's refuse. Maybe he was trying to protect her from further harm, in which case he must value her quite a bit to be willing to put up with the carpenters' noise and disorder.

But how much was that, she wondered, and then sighed, realizing that her conclusion was all supposition. His actual motives for finishing the remodeling might have nothing to do with her. Anyway, she already knew that he liked her. That he valued her both as a person and as a lover. And that was enough. Any deeper feeling would cause complications that she neither wanted nor needed, she told herself emphatically.

She had plans for her future. And a permanent relationship with a man didn't come into those plans for years yet. Not until she was firmly established in a good-paying job with a hefty bank account and had earned her Ph.D. Then she'd look around for an ideal mate. Someone who shared both her love of the classics and modern fiction. Definitely, not a description of Marcus Blackmore, she assured herself. She picked up her FORTRAN manual and began to study for her carefully planned future, which for some inexplicable reason, had begun to lose a lot of its appeal.

Cabin fever, she told herself firmly. Except for a quick visit to the doctor's yesterday, she'd been cooped up in the house since Saturday. Once she'd been out to lunch with Marcus, she'd feel better. She glanced at the clock. Three hours and he'd be here. A disquieting glow of happiness filled her and she resolutely began to read, trying to shut out the banging that wafted up from the first floor.

By one o'clock her mood of happy expectancy had dissipated, leaving a sense of bitter disappointment in its wake. She pressed her forehead against the glass of one of the huge windows and peered down at the pavement three floors below. There was still no sign of Marcus coming up the street. Finally she admitted to herself that he wasn't going to come. He hadn't been held up; he'd forgotten. Again. She gritted her teeth in frustration. She'd been so sure when he'd un-expectedly remembered her doctor's appointment yester-day that it signaled an improvement in his memory. But it hadn't. Apparently yesterday had been a lone miracle.

Ann limped over to the couch and sank down, pushing her FORTRAN book aside with an angry swipe. You could call him, she told herself. She eyed the phone sitting on his desk, but finally discarded the idea. She had more pride than to remind a man that he was supposed to be taking her out. Besides, Marcus was undoubtedly engrossed in his re-search and wouldn't appreciate being disturbed. As she ought to be engrossed in her studies, she lectured herself. She determinedly picked the FORTRAN book up. She'd wait another half hour before fixing herself a sandwich, in case Marcus did suddenly remember.

But he didn't and Ann spent a seemingly interminable afternoon trying to dredge up even the faintest interest in her studies. Between the noise from downstairs and her disappointment that Marcus had forgotten their date, it proved impossible and she finally gave up the effort, decid-ing to bake chocolate chip cookies instead.

After giving Jefferson a brief pat on the head, which he ignored in offended silence, and checking on Serendipity, who was peacefully cleaning his whiskers, she went down to the kitchen, pausing a moment to admire the walls going up in the living room. Ed was right. At this rate, they would be finished in a few weeks.

Mixing the cookie dough helped to relieve her unchar-acteristic restlessness, and by the time she'd taken the first batch out of the oven, she was feeling more her normal self.

She picked up a hot cookie and nibbled on it. It was de-licious. She hadn't lost her touch despite not having baked anything in well over a year. Marcus would love them. She slid another tray into the oven.

The carpenters had been gone almost an hour before Ann heard Marcus's key in the lock. She took her hands out of the dishwater and dried them on her apron. A feeling of contentment filled her. Marcus was home.

She hurried into the living room to find him eyeing the carpenters' handiwork with a resigned eye. Eagerly she searched the lean planes of his face, skimming over the laugh lines creasing his cheeks, the sharp blade of his nose, to come to rest on his firm lips. A hunger heated the air in her lungs and she slowly exhaled, wondering what he would do if she threw her arms around him and passionately kissed him. She wanted to. Desperately. It seemed like years since he'd kissed her and left for work, an eternity since he'd made love to her. Panic iced her mind at the thought that he might already be tired of her, but she steadfastly refused to even consider it. He didn't kiss her as if he was tired of her. Far from it. And the reason he probably hadn't made love to her was because of his concern over her foot.

"I see that pack of vandals showed up." He gestured toward the living room.

"They weren't so bad. As a matter of fact—" she grinned at him "—one of them can arch only one eyebrow."

"Oh?" Marcus dropped his briefcase on the floor and grabbed her, pulling her up against his broad chest. "But can he sneer sardonically?"

"Can anyone?" She laughed giddily as one corner of his mouth twisted strangely in a valiant attempt. "Besides, I thought the way to tell the hero was that he was the one who ravished the heroine."

"We'll give it a shot." Marcus's fingers dug deeply into her soft hips, pulling her lower body into his.

Ann shivered slightly, touching the tip of her tongue to the center of her upper lip and slowly running the palms of her hands up over his chest. The slightly springy texture of his body hair beneath the thin cotton of his knit shirt sent tremors of awareness traveling up her arms. She linked her hands behind his neck and flexed her fingers against his supple skin, relishing the texture of it.

Marcus's arms shifted upward and he crushed her to him, his mouth capturing her lips. There was nothing gentle about his kiss. It was as if his need of her was too great to allow time for the tender preliminaries, she thought disjointedly, and then ceased to think altogether as his tongue swept past the barrier of her teeth, plunging into her mouth. A shudder echoed through her body and she opened her mouth wider, straining into him, determined to distill the last ounce of pleasure from his kiss.

She moaned deep in her throat as the hardening warmth of his passion stoked her desire. She loved him so much. The fugitive thought trickled upward from her subconscious, gaining momentum as it richocheted through her disbelieving mind. She froze in his arms, instinctively denying the devastating burst of self-knowledge. She didn't love Marcus Blackmore. She couldn't! But she did and probably had for some time. The truth wouldn't be denied.

Marcus raised his head and tenderly cupped her cheeks in his palms, searching her pale face.

"Did I jar your foot?" he asked, sympathy coloring his voice.

She stared at him, trying to get a handle on the paroxysms of emotion churning through her. "Yes." She feebly clutched at the excuse he was offering. "Yes," she repeated, trying very hard to act normal.

"Don't worry." He released her with a final gentle kiss on the tip of her nose. "It should be completely better in another week or so.

Ann shook off the desolate feeling that feathered through her when he removed his arms.

"Unless you've damaged a nerve," he added meditatively.

She grimaced. "Don't give me a list of the gory options, I prefer not to know."

"Forewarned is forearmed."

"Forewarned is a lot more worry," she debated.

"With your imagination that's probably true. Why don't we go have some chocolate chip cookies instead?"

"How did you know I made them." She followed him into the kitchen.

"Elementary, my dear Watson. The whole house smells of chocolate. But more conclusively, you taste delicious. Just like a cookie." He got a half gallon of milk out of the refrigerator and poured himself a glass. "Want some?"

"No, thanks." A tender smile touched her lips as she watched him looking for the biggest cookie.

"Why don't you just eat two?" she suggested, going back to washing dirty pans.

"It's the principle of the thing. You always eat the biggest one first." He munched. "This is the best chocolate chip cookie I've ever had. You deserve a reward."

"Oh?" Her stomach did a flipflop; a reward offered intriguing possibilities.

"Uh-huh." Marcus reached for another one. "I'll take you with me tonight."

"With you?" she repeated in disappointment. She didn't want to go anywhere. She wanted to stay right here. Right here with Marcus.

"To the reception at the institute." He glanced at the clock. "It starts in a little over an hour. I only came home to change and pick you up."

"No, thank you," she said shortly. There was no way she was going to a social event at the institute. She didn't know the first thing about anything scientific. She'd wind up sounding like a fool. It wasn't that she was stupid. Or even uneducated. She probably knew more about the classics than all of them put together. Not that it would do her any good. What could she do? Print up a sign that said, "I may not have the vaguest idea what you're talking about, but I'm very knowledgeable about Greek and Latin"?

The thought was ridiculous. In a more normal setting she could try to work the conversation around to a neutral subject, but at the institute that would be impossible. They'd get started on an incomprehensible discussion about some obscure virus, and she'd be left standing there like an idiot. And Marcus would be ashamed of her. That horrible thought stiffened her resolve not to go.

"Why not?" Marcus broke into her frantic imaginings.

She tried a red herring. "I haven't anything to wear."

"It's informal. Wear that cream-colored dress that's hanging in the closet. You'll look even better than usual. As a matter of fact, a lot of people will be going directly from work."

She tried part of the truth. "Marcus, I clean the labs at that place. How can I socialize with them?"

"You mean that, simply because they make the messes that you clean up, you won't associate with them?"

"No, of course not!" She felt like crying at the censure in his eyes. "It's just that I'll feel out of place. I've never been to a cocktail party in my life. And I've never been very adroit at the social gatherings I have attended. And I won't know anyone."

"You'll know me. Please, Ann, I want you to come."

"All right," she capitulated, unable to resist his plea. But she very much feared that it was going to be a long evening.

To her surprise, the party was nowhere near as bad as she'd expected. Due mainly, she admitted, to Marcus's efforts. When they'd arrived at the institute, instead of leaving her at the door as she expected him to do, he'd put a possessive arm around her shoulder. But, still, he couldn't know how much she dreaded this affair. Even if she'd told him, he'd have had no patience with her fears. In her experience, men simply didn't.

"That dress looks even better on you than it did on the hanger." Marcus's eyes lingered on her small breasts jutting against the soft clinging fabric. "You look sleek and sensuous. And eminently touchable." His fingers lightly rubbed over her upper arm, helping to divert her mind from its worries.

"Thank you." Ann felt her spirits lift as she glanced down at her dress. It did look nice. Made of real silk, its clotted-cream color highlighted the ivory perfection of her skin and emphasized the gleaming lights in her shiny brown hair. Its deeply swirling cocktail-length skirt made her slender legs appear almost fragile, and the tucked bodice clung lovingly to her breasts.

She'd bought it last summer to attend the wedding of an acquaintance of hers from her married days. She'd spent much more on the dress than she could really afford, but the impulse to buy the silky creation had been irresistible. It was as if she was saying to Steve and all her old acquaintances that, in spite of their gloomy predictions at the breakup of her marriage, she was doing very well. The fact that she'd had to work six straight Saturdays to be able to afford the outfit had seemed a small price to pay.

"WOULD YOU LIKE SOMETHING to drink," Marcus asked. "The champagne punch is usually pretty good."

"No, thanks," she declined. "I don't want to risk winding up tipsy and doing something frightful."

"On what scale?"

"What do you mean, what scale?"

"Frightful by your standards? By my standards? Or by theirs?" He gestured around the crowded room.

"Isn't it basically the same thing?"

"Hardly. In the first place, you could never do anything frightful in my eyes." He looked thoughtful. "Stupid, perhaps. Inexplicable, definitely. But frightful, never." He smiled at her, warming her nervous heart. "You're much too kindhearted to ever knowingly hurt someone."

She recollected her lack of social skills. "How about embarrass them?"

"Embarrass? Well, I can't say as I've ever been embarrassed."

Ann believed him. He didn't seem bound by the same set of social rules as the rest of the world.

"And as for them—" He looked over the room thoughtfully. "If they survived what happened last year, a conventional little soul by the name of Ann Somerton is hardly likely to cause so much as a ripple."

"I am not a conventional little soul." She didn't like his description; it made her sound like goody twoshoes.

"I meant in public." Devilish little lights began to gleam in the depths of his blue eyes, and Ann felt an answering warmth flare to life deep within her. A totally inappropriate response, considering where they were. She shot a hasty glance around to see if his husky words had been overheard. A flush stained her pale cheeks as she realized the number of curious stares she was attracting.

"What happened last year?" she asked, more from a desire to change the subject than from any real wish to know.

"Michelangelo."

"Michelangelo what?"

"Not what, who. He was a sculptor. As hung up as you are on the past, I'd have expected you to already know that."

"I know who Michelangelo was," she said patiently. "But what I don't know is how he could affect an affair like this."

"It was his statue. More specifically, his sculpture of day from the tomb of Guiliano, Duca di Nemours. Although I suppose that a good portion of the blame has to go to the open bar," Marcus said reflectively.

"Is there a point to this story?" she asked, getting interested in spite of her nerves.

"I told you." He gave her a surprised glance. "It was Michelangelo. You see, we had this visiting researcher, Lorenzo Savonarola, from Rome, who was inordinately proud of anything even vaguely Italian."

"So? No one disputed Michelangelo's value as a sculptor, did they? Did you?" She cast him a suspicious look.

"Not me!" he declared emphatically. "It was Tricia Winston. She'd had one too many Scotch and sodas and kept insisting that Michelangelo was a terrible sculptor because his models are all posed in impossible positions."

"I seem to vaguely remember reading something about that." Ann said, frowning. "But why did that cause any trouble? I would have thought that it was a harmless enough topic of conversation at a cocktail party."

"Lorenzo took the criticism personally. And when his arguments failed to induce Tricia to change her mind, he decided to show her."

"Show her? But there's no statuary of any kind in the institute."

"Unfortunately. So Lorenzo did the only thing he could do. He positioned himself in exactly the same way as the statue, but Tricia still wouldn't give an inch. She insisted that it wasn't the same thing because Lorenzo was wearing a suit and the statue wasn't."

"Oh no!" Ann's eyes widened. "He didn't!"

"He did." Marcus nodded solemnly.

"I've heard of going to extremes to prove a point, but that's ridiculous."

"You sound remarkably like the director did. Except that he has a much more colorful vocabulary."

"Really?" She stole a covert glance at the rotund little leader of the institute. She'd never exchanged more than a brief good-evening with him, but she'd always felt he held himself above the rest of mankind. Somehow Marcus's revelations made him seem much more human.

Made them all seem more human. She swallowed a giggle. Nothing that interesting had ever happened at any of the company picnics she'd attended with Steve. Who would have expected something so uninhibited from a group of scientists. Although having met Marcus... Her eyes lingered on the breadth of his wide shoulders, lightly covered by his expertly tailored gray suit jacket.

"You know, Marcus, you'd make a superb subject for Michelangelo. You—"

"Marcus?" A deep voice interrupted them, and Ann glanced around to see a pleasant-looking middle-aged man bearing down on them. He didn't look familiar, but that was hardly surprising. Not only did she work nights, but most people tended to treat the cleaning staff as if they were invisible.

"Jim." Marcus turned Ann toward the man. "Ann, I'd like you to meet Jim Talbort. Jim, Ann Somerton. Jim's youngest son is very taken with the classics, although I think he's more interested in Latin than Greek."

"It's bloodier," Jim pointed out with distaste. "He lives and breathes the Gallic Wars. He intends to teach when he finally gets his Ph.D. Is that what you do?"

Ann recoiled. "No! I tried teaching my senior year and decided I'd rather starve than do it again."

"My sentiments exactly." A slightly built redhead joined their conversation.

Ann imperceptibly moved closer to Marcus. He introduced the redhead and her exquisitely dressed blond companion as Melissa and Elaine.

"I taught high school biology in Los Angeles before I landed a job here," continued the redhead. "I still have nightmares about it." She shuddered expressively. "One of my students said he was working on the ultimate germ-warfare weapon. And the really frightening thing was that he was incredibly smart. Not as smart as Marcus, though." She tossed a flirtatious glance at him, which he didn't seem to notice. "Thank heavens the institute rescued me. Although I still scan the papers every so often to see if Southern California has fallen victim to something awful."

"How could you tell?" Ann grinned, liking the woman in spite of her manner toward Marcus.

"Don't worry about Melissa," Elaine said. "She sees disaster under every stone."

"Under every microscope, darling!" Melissa laughed. "That's what comes with being an immunologist. Are you new here, Ann?"

"No." Ann forced herself to respond normally. "I've been working at the institute for almost a year now."

"You must really be dedicated to your research," Elaine said. "I can't remember seeing you before."

"That's because I work nights cleaning the labs."

"Oh?" Melissa appeared taken aback. Her eyes went from Ann to Marcus, who still had his arm around her.

"Why?" Jim asked. "Cleaning labs has nothing to do with Greek."

"True, but it pays the bills while I'm in school."

"I know exactly what you mean. My husband and I worked our way through college, taking any kind of job going," Elaine smiled reminiscently. "I still remember our first apartment. It was infested with millipedes so badly that at night when you turned a light on it looked like the walls were moving when they dashed for cover."

Ann shivered, visualizing the repulsive insects.

"I took to sleeping on my stomach," Elaine said, "because I was afraid my mouth would fall open in the night and one would drop in."

"You shouldn't be wasting your time cleaning labs for a pittance, Ann," Melissa said. "I had a roommate in grad school who worked as a cocktail waitress, and you wouldn't believe the money they pull down."

"No waitressing." Marcus's emphatic words momentarily stifled the conversation, and Ann could feel the speculative glances she was receiving at the possessive note in his voice. It was obvious that his collegues didn't know what to make of his attitude. Not that it was surprising, Ann thought ruefully. She didn't know what to make of it, either.

"If you'll excuse us." Marcus smiled at the group. "I want to introduce Ann to the director."

An hour later she was more than willing to fall in with Marcus's suggestion that they call it an evening. Her social smile felt pasted on, her head was throbbing and her foot ached ever so slightly.

"Does your foot hurt?" Marcus frowned down at her dress sandals, then turned to unlock his front door.

"It's just these three-inch heels," she groaned. "I'm not used to them." She stepped inside and slipped them off while Marcus closed the door behind them.

"Ah, that's better." She wiggled her toes on the cold marble of the entrance hallway.

"Hungry?" he asked.

"No." Ann started up the stairs, being careful where she stepped. One accident was more than enough. "The hors d'oeuvres weren't bad. Especially that clam dip. As a matter of fact, the whole event wasn't that bad. Most of your colleagues were quite nice."

"What did you expect?"

"Well, I guess I expected them to look down their noses at a lab cleaner, but they didn't." She bent to pat the sleepy-looking Jefferson who was waiting for them on the top floor. Of course, being Marcus's guest couldn't have hurt, she thought with a total lack of self-deceit. But whatever the reason, the evening had been a pleasant surprise. Marcus's world wasn't as closed as she'd originally thought. She could function in it. At least on a social level. Granted, there'd been times when they'd started to talk viruses and she'd been lost, but it hadn't been as bad as she'd expected. And there had been lots of general conversation in which she'd been able to join.

Although what good being able to interact socially with Marcus's associates was, she didn't know. An unhappy sigh escaped her. She wouldn't be here that much longer. He was bound to lose interest in her before too very long. The thought made her head droop.

"Tired?" He put his hands on her shoulders and pulled her back against his chest. Ann sagged into him, absorbing the taut feel of his thighs against her soft buttocks. She felt as if she wanted to grab at each opportunity to touch him. To store each memory against the long, lonely years ahead.

"Not really." She gasped when his hands slid down to cover her breasts. Longing tore through her body as he slowly kneaded.

"You could use an early night." He nuzzled the soft skin along the back of her neck, then moved upward to nibble on her ear lobe.

"Umm, Marcus," she purred. "That feels so good." She loved him so much. She wanted to tell him, but she didn't dare. Marcus hadn't asked for love. Nor had he offered it. He'd asked for friendship and a sexual relationship. And she loved him enough to want to give him what he wanted. Besides, she thought in some confusion, she didn't want the risks inherent in a more permanent relationship with a man as absentminded as Marcus.

Restlessly Ann turned in his arms and pressed herself against the hard, sinewy length of him, losing the thread of her disjointed thoughts in the hot glow of his eyes.

"Make love to me, Marcus Blackmore." The words simply popped out.

"Your wish is my command, my lovely." He swung her up in his arms and strode toward the bed. "I know just the thing to put new life into you."

He had, too. Ann stretched and snuggled against Marcus's relaxed body. The lingering sense of euphoric well-being that his lovemaking had engendered slowly seeped from her relaxed limbs. "I think you're onto a miracle cure." She traced languorous patterns on his chest.

Marcus captured her hand and began to kiss each separate finger. "Perhaps," he agreed. "But you do realize that before we publish, we'll have to do extensive testing." He dropped a kiss on the tip of her nose. "It also made me hungry." He bounded out of bed with an energy Ann envied, and pulled on a pair of jeans.

"Are there enough of those chocolate chip cookies to snack on?" he asked.

"Yes." She hid her disappointment when he zipped up his pants. She'd much rather have simply lay there in his arms than eat. "I made a double batch, so they'd last all week."

He looked crestfallen. "I can't have very many?"

"Of course you can," she relented. "I can always make more. Bring me a few, too, please," she called after him.

He was back in five minutes with a tray bearing a huge stack of cookies and two glasses of milk.

"Here." He handed her the tray, slipped out of his jeans and slid back under the sheets.

"You can't eat cookies in bed," she objected, hurriedly holding up the tray as Jefferson, smelling food, bounded onto the bed.

"For pity's sake!" She eyed the frankly begging dog with disfavor.

"You can give him one. I brought plenty."

"It's the principle of the thing," she objected. "Dogs don't eat cookies."

"That's ridiculous." Marcus handed him one. "Of course he eats cookies. Look at him."

"I meant that he shouldn't eat them!"

"Neither should humans, come to that."

"And you'll get crumbs in the bed," she added.

"Then read a book while you eat. All the crumbs will land in the pages." He handed her her copy of Greek mythology from the nightstand. "I wanted to see what happened anyway."

"Happened where?" she asked.

"In *Ten Little Indians*. I'm pretty sure I know who did it."

"Hallelujah! You mean I finally found something you liked to read?" She fell back against the pillows in mock astonishment, and the sheet slipped off her bare breasts.

His eyes darkened perceptibly as he studied the pale mounds, and Ann felt desire well within her despite the perfection of what they'd shared a few minutes ago.

"And do." He reached out and gently covered her warm flesh.

She forced herself to act calmly. "You liked the book?"

"Well, mysteries aren't too bad," he conceded absently, his thumb lightly grazing the hardening tip of her breast.

She leaned into the warm pressure of his hand. "They're kind of like research. And speaking of research—" He plucked the glass of milk from her hand and set it on the bedside table, then pulled her unresisting body into his. Ann went willingly, not even noticing when the cookies tumbled into the sheets, scattering crumbs everywhere.

12

ANN CONTEMPLATED the six slices of bacon in the pan, weighed Marcus's appetite and added six more. She flipped the burner on and turned toward the heavy tread of Marcus's feet in the hallway. A sense of rightness enveloped her as soon as he entered the kitchen.

Welcomingly, her eyes sketched the broad planes of his body before homing in on his face. His curly black hair was still damp from his shower, and a renegade curl had tumbled down into the center of his broad forehead. She watched in fascination as his long brown fingers impatiently swept it back. She began to remember the feel of those fingers gently exploring the soft secret places of her body last night. A soft melting warmth began to flow with drugged insistence through her.

After a week of sharing his life and his lovemaking, the fascination he held for her was growing by leaps and bounds. Closer exposure to Marcus hadn't sated her initial attraction. It had deepened and widened it into an all-encompassing love. She'd discovered additional facets of his personality that intrigued her. To her unease, her love was growing at a rate that threatened to take over her entire life.

"Good morning, Ann." His greeting brought her out of her reverie and she smiled at him, watching as he flung his briefcase on the countertop, narrowly missing the orange juice.

He walked over to her and gave her a seemingly absent
peck on the cheek, but instead of withdrawing as she'd
expected, his lips lingered, moving lightly over her cheekbone. A shiver chased over her skin at the caress. She welcomed the heat from his body reaching out to her.

"Hmmm." He continued his evocative exploration. "You
taste so good and you feel like—" he paused meditatively
"—like a soft, velvety mold."

"Benign, I hope," she whispered breathlessly.

"I think you're a catalyst," he muttered, his tongue flick-
ing lightly into her ear.

"A catalyst?" She twisted slightly under the impact of his
caress.

"Yes." Marcus speared his fingers through her hair and
turned her head up, his eyes focusing intently on her softly
parted lips. "You cause all kinds of things to happen, but you
basically remain unchanged yourself."

"Oh?" she murmured without any real interest. Her concentration was focused wholly on his mouth. She wanted
so badly to kiss him. She paused, blinked to clear her passion-fogged mind and sniffed as a pungent odor began to
impress itself on her senses.

"What do I smell burning?"

"Probably me." He chuckled. "You do very illogical
things to my internal temperature gage."

"Thank you. I think." She grinned up into his smiling
face. "But . . ." An angry sputter from the stove suddenly
enlightened her as to the problem.

"The bacon!" She whirled around and hurriedly yanked
the pan off the burner. "It's ruined." She glared down at the
shriveled bits as though it were all their fault. She'd so
wanted to send Marcus off to work with a nutritious breakfast. Now she'd ruined it.

"Don't worry." He dropped a final kiss on her shiny hair. "Bacon's loaded with cholesterol."

"And you don't eat bacon because its high in cholesterol!" Ann stared at him. "You, the undisputed king of the fast-food chains!"

"I didn't say I didn't eat it," he replied reasonably. "I merely pointed out that cholesterol was bad for you."

"Oh." She wondered if he'd been attempting to comfort her. Getting out a clean glass pan, she put out more bacon and, this time, threw it in the microwave. She set the timer and, as she waited, considered his reaction to having his breakfast postponed. Her experience with her ex-husband had led her to believe that men were short-tempered over delays in the morning. But Marcus certainly wasn't. She glanced tenderly at him. He was sipping his orange juice and glaring at the computer printout by his plate as if it were an insect carrying an infectious disease.

"What's that?" he demanded ominously.

"That's a harbinger of things to come. No, don't reject it out of hand," she added hurriedly when he opened his mouth.

"Look at it and I mean really look. I took that report on the very bottom of your desk and fed everything into the computer and then I asked it questions."

"Questions?"

"Yes. Of course the answers are of limited value to you because I don't know enough about your work to even know what questions to ask. But the point is, that program I wrote will collate information at an astonishing rate. For example, notice the chart showing distribution of skin cancer among swimmers, surfers and sunbathers in their twenties, thirties and forties."

"Mmm." He began to really read the printout.

"Marcus?" she asked hesitantly. "Just how dangerous is strong sunlight?"

"Not very, and not at all in moderation," he answered absently. "It's like that bacon. Cholesterol can cause problems, but that doesn't mean it will."

"I see. Was that report something you did?"

"No, they're working on this down in Washington. I'm merely keeping abreast of things."

"Well, what about my program?" She took the bacon out of the microwave.

"It has possibilities," he admitted grudgingly. "If I could trust that damned computer not to . . ." His voice trailed off and he stared at the kitchen cabinets, obviously lost in thought.

Satisfied, Ann set his breakfast in front of him and slipped onto the stool beside him. She hadn't expected him to do an abrupt about-face and suddenly embrace computers. It was enough that he'd seen the possibilities. Later she'd push to consolidate her position.

"Do you really like doing this?" He gestured toward the printout. "Are you happy with the thought of spending the rest of your life putting information into some machine?"

"Happy is a relative term," she responded seriously. "I'll certainly be happier working with computers than cleaning out labs. And a lot better paid, too."

"But you love your Greek," he accused.

"True," she sighed. "In an ideal world, I'd be able to spend all my time simply studying it. But this isn't an ideal world. Don't let it bother you," she said when he frowned. "Working with computers isn't perfect, but it's something I can live with."

"For the rest of your life?"

"For the rest of my working life," she corrected, momentarily chilled by the picture of a bleak future without him, which his words had called up. "We aren't all as lucky as you are, Marcus. To be able to spend our time doing exactly what we want to do."

"I am lucky." His eyes roamed over her soft face. "Very, very lucky. And I'm also going to be late." He suddenly became brisk. "What's your class schedule today?"

"I'm through at one."

"I could pick you up at school, and we could have lunch together."

"I'd love lunch, but why don't we meet back here? That way I can walk Jefferson before we go," she alibied. That way, if he forgot all about her, she wouldn't be left standing in front of the school for hours.

"Fine." He polished off his eggs. "The backyard should be completely cleared by next week, according to the construction company."

"It's amazing how fast they work. The second floor is virtually done."

"I know. The architect mentioned it when he called yesterday. He wants me to let that idiot woman come back."

"Idiot woman?"

"The one who decorated the basement without telling me first."

"Oh, that idiot woman."

"Anyway, I told him to ask you and see what you said."

"What's to say? She did a beautiful job downstairs. I think you ought to let her have a go at finishing off the bedrooms."

"One bedroom," Marcus corrected. "Only the master bedroom. Leave the others alone."

"Finances?" she asked sympathetically.

"No, bitter experience," he replied darkly. "If you have spare bedrooms, people come to visit and they stay. And not only do they stay, but they move things."

"Ah, the ultimate sin." She nodded sagely. "You know, Marcus, what you ought to do is simply wire your desk and zap anyone deranged enough to touch it."

"I wonder if I could?" he mused.

"Marcus, I was being snide."

"Oh, not a nasty jolt. Merely a slight shock." His eyes were lit with enthusiasm. "Like an electric fence."

"Marcus. The wonder isn't that people touch your stuff, but that they ever visit you in the first place!"

"You came. And you stayed," he said smugly.

Ann looked at him in exasperation, wondering what he'd say if she told him that she'd stayed because she loved him. He'd probably run a mile, she thought morosely. An affair was one thing, but a declaration of love was quite another.

"Don't look so sad." He placed a warm, coffee-flavored kiss on her lips. "I promise I won't wire my desk if you don't like the idea. Have a good morning, and don't forget that we're meeting back here for lunch."

"You, too." She kissed him back, reluctant to break the contact. "Ah, the construction crew is here." She withdrew at the sound of Jefferson in a frenzy hurtling himself against the front door. "Drat, I forgot to shut him up in the bedroom."

"You do that while I escape out the back door." He grabbed his briefcase and hurried out. "See you at one," he called back over his shoulder.

By the time one o'clock came, Ann was tired, hot and her foot ached. The morning had seemed endless, and she was eagerly looking forward to an icy drink followed by a cool shower. She let herself into the house, pausing briefly. Silence greeted her. Curiously, she wandered through the first floor, looking for the carpenters. She didn't find them. What she did find was a note saying that some necessary materials hadn't arrived and they had left to track them down and wouldn't be back till morning.

"I'm coming," she called. The faint sound of yapping reached her ears. She dropped her books on the steps and hurried upstairs to get Jefferson for his walk, hoping he'd be quick about it. He wasn't. He insisted on investigating every step and crack in the sidewalk for two solid blocks before she could induce him to return.

"Life is going to be much simpler once they get the back-yard cleaned up," she told the wiggling little dog, taking off his lead. Jefferson ignored her, running off to sniff all the places that the carpenters had dared to touch that morning.

"Crazy beast," she said affectionately, then wandered out to the kitchen to open a Coke. As she'd feared, Marcus wasn't there. She checked the time. One-thirty. There was still time for him to remember. She took a long, satisfying swallow of her drink and went upstairs. She decided to take a quick shower. The ride on the packed bus in the ninety-degree heat had made her feel as if she'd been in a sauna.

The shower revived her, and she wrapped the towel around herself and wandered back into the bedroom, coming to a surprised halt at the sight of Marcus standing in front of the chest of drawers. An almost nude Marcus. She breathlessly noted the fact that he was wearing only a pair of white briefs and one navy sock. Clean underwear and a pile of socks littered the floor beside him.

He must have taken a shower in one of the bathrooms on the bedroom level, she realized when a fugitive droplet of water trickled off a tendril of his black hair to slide down over his deeply tanned back.

"I can't find it," he complained.

"Your missing sock?" She clutched the towel more tightly around her, shivering slightly as the room's air-conditioning chilled her still-damp skin.

"Yes." He tossed another handful of clean underwear out of the drawer.

Ann sighed as it fluttered to the floor. She hurried over to the chest and hastily pushed him aside, trying not to notice the way her arm burned where it had brushed up against his chest. She pulled open the third drawer, looking for the pairs of socks she'd washed. Sure enough, they were there.

She gestured. "Take your pick."

"I have." His voice was a soft purr. "You." He suddenly whipped off the damp towel, and Ann gasped in surprise. His hand cupped her chin, and he tilted her face upward.

"But your socks..." she murmured, becoming distracted by his eyes. They seemed to glow under the force of his passion, and she could feel the now-familiar heaviness settling deep in her abdomen.

"You smell so good." His thumb rubbed lightly over her jawline. "Like violets. The large purple kind you find in the woods in the springtime. And your mouth..." His thumb moved to rub lightly over her lower lip, then slipped inside.

"It begs to be kissed," he whispered seductively. His hands slipped around her head, holding it steady while his lips covered hers. His tongue aggressively plunged inside in joyful anticipation of pleasures yet to be tasted.

Ann moaned deep in her throat and pressed closer to him. She loved him so much it was almost painful. And she wanted to express that love in the most basic way possible. She wanted to absorb him into her. To impress herself on his mind so deeply that he'd never lose interest in her. Desperation lent her courage and she encircled his lean waist with her arms. She felt a compulsive need to show Marcus how much she loved him even if she couldn't risk actually saying the words aloud. But she could hardly swing him up in her arms as he did her.

"What's wrong, Ann?" Marcus looked deeply into her troubled eyes, which widened with pleasure when his hand cupped her breast. His thumb gently rasped over the responsive nipple. "Would you rather not?"

"Not?" she queried distractedly, pressing herself against his hand.

"Not make love now."

"No! Oh, no." Ann forced herself to meet his eyes. "I want to very much." She moistened her dry lips when his hand flattened against her aching breast, and he slowly rotated his callused palm over her throbbing flesh. "In fact, I want to do to you what you're doing to me," she blurted out in a rush. "I want to explore every inch of your body. To kiss all of you."

"Then why don't you?" His voice was infinitely gentle.

"I wasn't sure what you'd think of the idea," she confessed candidly.

"For such an intelligent woman, you have some very strange ideas."

She drew courage from the indulgent expression on his face. "The thing is," she confided, "I can't think of a good way to get you from here to the bed."

"Just take my hand and lead me. I'd follow you anywhere." His face suddenly assumed a serious expression, but she was too busy dealing with what was actually happening to catch hidden meanings.

She picked up his large hand and threaded her fingers through his, wishing she possessed the power to enmesh herself in the fabric of his life so easily. She tugged him down onto the bed and, putting her hands on his chest, gently pushed him backward. Marcus crossed his arms behind his head and smiled enticingly at her.

"I'm waiting to be seduced."

Ann took a deep breath and blanked out all her fears, allowing her love for Marcus to fill her mind to the exclusion of all else. She studied his magnificent body from beneath half-closed lids with the intensity of a child let loose in a candy shop and unsure of where to start. Her attention landed on his firm lips, and she swayed toward them as if drawn by a magnet.

She touched his cheeks, following the deep crease in them down to his jawline. His emerging beard rasped over her skin, sending shivers through her. Slowly, savoring each precious second, she explored his face with her fingertips, passing along the line of his high cheekbones, tracing over his nose and lightly outlining the flying line of his black brows. Lovingly she delved into the firm swirls of his ears, barely noticing his body's convulsive jerk at her action.

Heat from his supple flesh seeped into her fingers, radiating along her nerve endings to the farthest reaches of her body. Slowly she exhaled a shaky breath and leaned over him. Her lips touched softly on his jawline, then moved downward, nuzzling his supple skin, and her tongue dipped into the hollow at the base of his neck.

The taste of him filled her mouth. Her breathing was becoming constricted, and her heartbeat developed an uneven cadence that reflected the confused state of her mind. She placed her hands flat on his chest, flexing her fingers in the wiry hair that covered him. His muscles rippled at her action and Ann absorbed the motion, allowing it to flow into her.

Fascinated with his physical makeup, she flicked the tips of his flat, masculine nipples with her nails, glorying in the involuntary gasp that escaped him. She lowered her head and lightly traced down the center of his chest with the tip of her tongue, watching his fists clench under the force of his reaction.

"You have the most beautiful body, Marcus," she said raptly, continuing her tracing above the elastic on his shorts. "I know that you aren't supposed to use that term for men, but in your case it applies."

"Thank you," he rasped.

Boldly she slipped her fingers under his waistband, vaguely surprised at her own daring. She laid her cheek on his flat belly and peered up at him through passion-fogged eyes.

"Do you mind if I take off your shorts?" She let her fingers stray lower to grasp his hot, pulsating masculinity.

"Oh, hell!" Marcus jackknifed up. "I'm sorry, Ann, but you're too damned good at the seduction bit. I can't wait any longer."

He flipped her on her back and, stripping off his shorts, crouched above her.

"Like time payments." Distracted at the sight of his aroused body, she spoke absently.

"Or heaven," he corrected equally absently. His large hand covered her abdomen, and she gasped at the torrent of sensation pouring through her. She wanted him. Wanted everything he had to give.

She vocalized her need. "Make love to me, Marcus. Now."

"Yes." Marcus moved against her, filling her with a powerful surge of his body.

A soft, whimpering sound clogged the back of her throat as she absorbed his hardness.

"That's right, Ann." His hands moved her legs, positioning them around his waist, and she clenched him to her with no thought of the demands she was making on him. She was beyond rational thought, beyond everything but an elemental response to the passion that deepened at every thrust of his body. She flung back her head, her breath coming in short gasps and her whole mind centered on the pathway to ecstasy, drawing her inexorably down.

At last the storm broke, hurtling her into a world of sensation. She barely heard Marcus or noticed when he collapsed on her boneless body. It was minutes before she slowly began to surface from the sensual maelstrom that had engulfed her. It was minutes before she became aware of such mundane details as Marcus's heavy body sprawled contentedly across her.

Tenderly she stroked his thick black hair and ran soothing fingers over his sweat-slickened shoulders. Her love for him was so strong it seemed to have a life of its own.

"Thank you, Marcus."

He levered himself up on one elbow and dropped a final kiss on her soft lips.

"I'm sorry I couldn't last the whole seduction. We'll have to give it a second shot when I get back." He stood up and looked around for his clothes.

Lovingly her eyes followed his movements. He was magnificant standing there, naked except for one navy sock.

"Back from where?" She rolled over on her stomach and watched him walk to the bureau. "If you're looking for socks, they're still in the third drawer."

He grunted in satisfaction as he extracted a pair. "To Washington."

"Washington!" A sense of dread filled her. Marcus was going away.

"Uh-huh. I have to go check on something at the National Institute of Health. I only came home to change and to warn you that I'll be late."

"You're not staying over?" she asked, relief percolating through her.

"No." He glanced at the clock. "I should be able to make the three-o'clock shuttle to Washington, but I'm not sure exactly what flight I'll be back on. I'll call you from the airport before the plane takes off."

"I won't be here," she reminded him. "I'm supposed to go back to work tonight."

"Oh, yes. I meant to tell you about that." His words were muffled as he pulled on a powder-blue knit shirt. "I resigned your job for you yesterday. Effective immediately," he added as an afterthought.

"You did what?" She jerked up and stared at him in horror.

"I said I resigned—"

"I heard that!" she snapped.

"Then why did you ask?" He calmly pulled on a pair of gray pants.

Ann took a deep, steadying breath. "What I meant was, how could you resign my job!" Despite her efforts, her voice rose with the strength of her indignation.

He took her question literally. "I called personnel and told them."

"Marcus," she began, trying to keep the panic and anger coursing through her out of her voice. "I need that job. It's the only one that I could find that had regular night hours, paid enough to cover my expenses and that I was qualified to do."

"You don't need it now. You can stay home and study your Greek instead. Or, better still, you can go back to school in the fall and start on your Ph.D. If you really want a job, you can help me with those damned computers."

Ann closed her ears to the tempting words. All the more alluring because it was exactly what she wanted to do. To be free to study her Greek and yet still feel like she was making an important contribution by helping Marcus with his information-processing problems. He fastened his belt and looked around for his shoes, finding them half-hidden under the bed. "I'm perfectly capable of supporting a wife."

"A wife!" she gasped.

"Of course we're going to get married. We belong together. Have you seen what I did with that blue folder?"

"To hell with the blue folder!" she ground out through clenched teeth.

"If what's in it is true, I agree with you. Ah, there it is." He kicked aside a pile of socks and picked it up. "I'll try not to be too late." He dropped a kiss on her mussed hair. "I can't guarantee it, though. And don't go wandering around after dark by yourself."

"Marcus!" Ann yelled at him as he started down the stairs. "You can't simply drop a bombshell like this and then fly off to Washington. I need that job. It allows me to be independent."

He paused at the top of the steps. "You worry too much about money."

"Of course I do!" she snapped. "It's because I haven't any. I told you that it's only when you've got more than you need that you can afford to ignore it."

"An interesting philosophic point." He momentarily looked thoughtful. "But I haven't time to debate it now. Take care." He bounded down the stairs.

"I don't believe this. I don't believe any of this," she sniffed unhappily. "Things were going so well, and he had to go and do that." Panic filled her. She needed that job. It was her ticket to the future. But what future would she have without Marcus? The appalling prospect chilled her.

"Oh, hell." Ann distractedly ran her fingers through her hair and firmly resisted the impulse to indulge in a hearty bout of tears. She didn't need any more emotionalism; she needed to think. And she would, she declared to herself firmly. Just as soon as she made a pot of coffee.

Twenty minutes later, she was sitting at the kitchen counter with a steaming mug of coffee in her hand, staring at a blank sheet of paper. Purposefully she drew a line down the middle and wrote at the top of the right-hand side, "For" and, on the left, "Against."

Of its own volition, her hand went to the right side and wrote "I love him" at the top of the page. She loved his dry sense of humor, the endearing way he tried to look after her, his sharp intelligence, his single-mindedness, his loyalty, his very real kindheartedness, the fact that he really cared about people and expressed that concern in a positive way. She remembered the old woman who'd owned Jefferson. Halfway down the page, Ann stopped writing, realizing that her list of reasons for loving Marcus could fill ten pages, and that still wouldn't solve anything. Her love for him wasn't the problem.

It was the official seal of permanence that he wanted to put in their relationship that was. He wanted her to give up her financial independence and rely totally on him. A sense of panic welled up in her. She'd done that once, and it had been an unmitigated disaster. She expelled her breath on a deep sigh, trying very hard to calm her skittering nerves. Think, don't react, she told herself.

Determinedly, she reviewed her first marriage, trying to see it objectively. The problem hadn't been with her marriage per se, she realized. It had been that neither she nor Steve had been mature enough to make a marriage work. They'd jumped into it for all the wrong reasons. She'd wanted to escape a home life, where she'd felt like an interloper, and he'd wanted to marry someone because his mother had died and he was lonely. Even so, they might have made a success of it, if they'd felt anything more for each other than a rather tepid affection.

And a lot of it had been her fault. For the first time Ann fully accepted her share of the blame. Instead of trying harder to solve their problems, she'd retreated into her studies, further widening the already substantial gulf between them. She'd always seen their problems strictly in terms of their constantly precarious financial situation, but it had been much more basic that that, she admitted. They had had nothing in common. Absolutely nothing except having gone to high school together.

Thoughtfully she nibbled the end of her pencil. She and Marcus had lots of things in common, but the most important one was that they were both mature adults with a passion for learning as well as for each other.

What it all boiled down to was a question of trust. Did she trust him enough to allow him financial control of her life?

A vision of Marcus gently bending over her injured foot came to her mind. Followed by the memory of the way he stayed by her side at the cocktail party, helping her to find her feet among his colleagues. When she'd really need him, he'd been there without her having to say anything. That was the important thing. Not his annoying habit of forgetting luncheon dates. He'd undoubtedly always do that, but it wasn't really important. She was mature enough and had a positive enough self-image that she could cope with being forgotten without taking it as a rejection of herself as a person.

Happiness began to swell within her. She found it impossible to regret the loss of her cleaning job. It had served its purpose. She'd proved to herself that she could control her own life. That she could shape her own future. She wasn't sacrificing that future by agreeing to marry Marcus. She was enriching it beyond her wildest dreams.

"How could you ever have hesitated, you fool?" she berated herself, glancing down at the sheet with all its reasons for and none against. Just as soon as Marcus got home, she was going to throw her arms around him and accept.

Unfortunately, it didn't turn out to be that easy. Shortly after six o'clock a secretary from Washington called to relay the information that Marcus had run into problems and wouldn't be home until sometime the next day.

Filled with frustration, Ann hung up the phone. She wanted to shout her acceptance of his proposal from the rooftops, and she couldn't even share it with the man involved. But she could share it with a friend. A pleased smile lit her face. She'd promised to let Gladys know when she'd be returning to work. Instead she'd call and tell her that she wouldn't be returning. That she was going to marry Marcus.

Better yet, Ann decided, glancing at the clock. She had plenty of time to get to the institute before Gladys took her seven-o'clock coffee break. Ann laughed aloud, utterly happy. She could hardly wait to share her wonderful news. She grabbed her purse and headed for the door. The visit with Gladys would help to pass this evening, and tomorrow—she paused to savor the joyful anticipation—tomorrow she'd accept Marcus's proposal.

By the next day Ann's mood of happy expectancy had evaporated. In the back of her mind was the very real fear that he might forget he'd ever proposed.

Finally, at three-thirty, Jefferson started barking. A cab was drawing up in front of the house. Ann took a deep, calming breath and hurried downstairs. She found Marcus in the front hall, fending off a deliriously happy dog. She knew exactly how the dog felt.

"Hi." She smiled at Marcus, the strength of her feelings showing clearly in her eyes. Now that he was here, she was suddenly beset with uncertainties. Should she blurt out an acceptance or try to lead up to it?

Marcus took the decision out of her hands.

"I missed you," he said simply. "Here, these are for you." He handed her a manila envelope.

"What is it?" She opened it, curious about its contents.

"My stock portfolio. I called my accountant while I was in Washington and told him to transfer it to you. I picked it up on the way back from the airport. It's not a fortune, but it'll keep you in comfort if anything happens to me."

"Oh, Marcus." Ann felt tears prick her eyes. "I've been waiting since yesterday to tell you how much I love you. I don't need this to convince me to marry you." She sniffed. "I finally figured out that real security isn't money. It's the love I feel for you. That'll always be there for me to draw strength from. No matter what else happens."

"And the love I feel for you." He pulled her into the circle of his arms.

"You love me?" she questioned shyly. She'd known he liked her. That he respected her as well as desired her, but she hadn't dared to allow herself to hope that he loved her.

"Of course I love you!" He looked at her in surprise. "I think I've loved you from the beginning."

"The very beginning?" She snuggled her face into his neck.

"Well, maybe not from the very beginning," he said reflectively. "At first, my feelings were a little more basic than that. You have a very distracting body, you know. But once I actually started to talk to you, I found out that there was a whole lot more to you than merely a beautiful face and a glorious shape."

"Oh?" she prompted.

"Uh-huh." Marcus nuzzled her ear. "There was your kindheartedness to Serendipity, your intelligence, your willingness to work for what you wanted, your tenacity, even your clumsiness was endearing."

"I am not clumsy," she muttered.

"I found myself wanting to take care of you. To give you happy memories to replace your sad ones."

"Oh, Marcus," she sighed. "It's scary that I'm so happy. But I want you to put those stocks back in your name." She looked up into his eyes, her heart twisting at the love she saw reflected there.

"How about if I put both our names on them?"

"Fine, you can call your accountant just as soon as we've finished."

"Finished?"

"Yes." Ann smiled at him, drawing confidence from his love. "I only got to explore half of you the last time, and I hate to leave things half done."

"But have you considered the variables," he said in all seriousness.

"Variables?" she whispered. Her line of thought wavered as the insidious magic of his body started to influence her receptive senses.

"Any good researcher knows that you have to control variables. Now last time we made love you were wearing nothing but the most delicious scent."

"And you were wearing one navy sock." A brilliant joy illuminated her eyes. "So we'll have to try all the different clothing variations."

"To say nothing of the locale." He nodded encouragingly. "I know this perfect little inn in Maine we can visit."

"This is beginning to sound like a lifetime research project." He swept her off her feet and into his arms, and she snuggled against him.

"That's what I had in mind," he replied tenderly, starting up the stairs.

Harlequin Temptation

COMING NEXT MONTH

#121 THE VITAL INGREDIENT
Mary Jo Territo

Terry couldn't believe Tony Mangione was a thief. But it appeared the persuasive macaroni magnate had stolen more than her heart....

#122 ON LOVE'S TRAIL Judith Arnold

Any large, friendly stranger who gave her black-eyed Susans couldn't be all bad. And Cliff made sure Gretchen felt very *good* about inviting him to share her tent....

#123 DESERT RAIN Regan Forest

Keith was keeping something from Laura—a secret that threatened to turn the oasis of their love to dust. But then the rain came....

#124 THE HOMING INSTINCT
Elizabeth Glenn

Throwing over a dazzling soap career wasn't easy for Kelly—nor was going home again. Her reunion with hunky Matt Kendall, her high school heartthrob, made it all worthwhile....

Take 4 novels and a surprise gift FREE